BY VERCORS

THE SILENCE OF THE SEA
THREE SHORT NOVELS:
Guiding Star
Night and Fog
The Verdun Press

THREE SHORT NOVELS

THREE SHORT NOVELS

BY VERCORS

Little, Brown and Company · Boston · 1947

CONTENTS

GUIDING STAR

A TRANSLATION BY ERIC SUTTON

OF *La Marche à l'Etoile*

BY VERCORS

I. FAITH AND LIGHT

Reason can reach further than madness.
And what is more reasonable than, first of all,
to seek the Kingdom of God, and His Justice?

— PAUL CLAUDEL, *Saint Louis*

> Only in one way can you be sure of having found your place in life, and that is by the attainment of a point from which, quite literally, you cannot move.
> — PAUL CLAUDEL, *Saint Louis*

THE END OF LOVE is nearly always sordid. Sometimes lovers kill their love; and then its death is horrible. Thus perished Othello's under the dark assaults of jealousy. How fatal was his blunder in accusing Desdemona! The heart shudders and revolts at the very thought.

Where lies the blame for what happened to Thomas? Who slew his love and his life? Who sent him to his death with his soul in ruins? Was France to blame? No, it was a lie that did that deed. And it was a hideous blunder too, that brings the tears into my eyes — tears not of pity but of wrath.

୶

I was little more than a boy when I first knew him. Indeed as far back as I can remember, he figures in my recollections. The story I have to tell

5

is one that I learned by degrees, and in disconnected episodes. My task has been to bring them all together, and I realize that nothing is more difficult than to depict a man one knows too well. At what point shall the tale begin?

Shall I take the easy way known as the time-sequence? A convenient method, but rather devoid of art. Not indeed that art is needed for my purpose. Heaven deliver me from it!

The story starts a long way back, and what I know of it is scanty. It begins with a conversion — an ancestor who became a Bishop. An ambitious man, no doubt, who found the presence of his heretic family irksome. One can well imagine the unctuous, merciless pressure that drove the Muritz family from the glass foundries of the Vosges, where it originated, to those of Bohemia, whither it migrated. The Bishop's nephew married a girl from Brünn and founded a dynasty. About 1860 one of the great-grandsons appears at Pressburg as a well-to-do shipowner, with a fleet of lighters plying up and down the Danube. France is far away, and — it would seem — forgotten. The women, like their families, spoke German and Czech (or Hungarian, or Slovak) ; but the boys, from father to son, learned to speak French on equal terms with all their other languages. The shipowner had one son only, and six daughters. The daughters spoke Slovak and German. The son, in accordance with tradition, spoke French as well. His name was Thomas.

He was twelve years old in 1878, when his father died. The seven women of the Muritz family came upon a difficult time. The mother sold the Pressburg establishment, and they all settled down to a very restricted life in the old house at Devîn. Gradually the daughters married. It was one of Thomas's uncles who bought the shipping business, and when Thomas left school he was to have joined him. But the old house at Devîn decided otherwise.

The old house, do I say? It was in fact the turret room at the southwest corner, with high windows through which the setting sun gleamed on gilded leather bindings. It is there that this history begins. In that room was born the enduring ardor, the devouring love, that dwelt in the heart of Thomas Muritz, and only left him, in a moment of horrible revulsion, when life left him also.

త్ళ

It was there, among those serried bookshelves, that Madame Muritz found Thomas more often

than he should have been. She used to be angry, but
at heart she was delighted. She herself read little,
but she was glad that her son was so bookish. It
did not enter her mind that this passion of his was
to take him from her, and so soon.

Half the books in the library were German and
half were French. Thomas read both with fluency.
"Flat on the floor in front of the porcelain stove
was the way he always used to read," said his uncle
to me — that was the vision of Thomas that lingered
in his mind nearly half a century later. The Czech
Government had sent him on a mission to France
to discuss traffic problems — it was the first time he
had been there since the war. I watched him sipping his glass of brandy (brandy from my own
grapes) with the air of a connoisseur. "Always like
that, flat on the floor, each time I went to see his
mother. If I ever saw him otherwise, I don't remember it." His free hand, a small plump hand,
indicated in an expressive little gesture his failure
to remember. Only his hands had any expression.
His large face, much too large for his squat and
aging person, was the face of a man always half
asleep. He smiled a Buddha-like smile.

"I daresay you think it funny" — he talked not
without a certain heavy eloquence in a shamelessly

execrable French — "that he should have had these tastes for literature; that he goes on reading to this day, though he'll be sixty soon — and that he still likes Alexandre Dumas? But I rather doubt whether you understand." His large eyes fixed me with an ironic stare from beneath his heavy eyelids. "Dumas? Nonsense — it wasn't Dumas. It was . . . it was France!" He drained his glass and closed his eyes, savoring the last drop. "He is a truly faithful person, and fidelity is not a matter for laughter," he went on, and gravely fixed his eyes upon me. "You see, I didn't quite understand in those old days. . . . I didn't understand that he wasn't reading Alexandre Dumas . . . he was reading the history of France. There was no history of France at Devîn, except Thiers's *Revolution,* and besides he was then a boy of thirteen. But . . ." And he lifted three fingers, merely to indicate that he was dropping this subject in favor of another. "You have never heard of Bölöni in France, of course . . . Alexandre Farkas Bölöni . . . *The Quest for Liberty.* . . . Well — " He paused, and smacked his lips like a fish emitting a bubble. "When I recall that it was I who gave him that book! — Bölöni, you must know, went off in quest of liberty. Went off — mark you." He laughed, and as he did so his great person quivered, though not a muscle of his face moved. "And Gilbert, too, went off, in *Joseph Balsamo,* do you remember? The splendid, dashing Gilbert. On foot, to Paris." He pointed a plump finger at me, waggling it to emphasize his points. "Went off, on foot, to Paris. That, of course, wouldn't have been enough. There was that fellow Hugo as well. Hugo! There he used to lie, flat on the floor in front of the porcelain stove, devouring Hugo day after day, not to mention Alexandre Dumas, Balzac, and Eugène Sue. What a medley! . . . You said to me that it was odd that he should still like all that stuff, just as it came along. In the first place, it didn't just come along, those names were to him enveloped in a sort of sanctity. But — it's mainly because you didn't know him when he was young and enthusiastic. . . . 'The Mysteries of Paris': France, Justice and Liberty. All that meant something, you know, to a young man from the Danube. He never forgot, because he is naturally loyal." He burst into a sudden laugh, a real laugh this time, and his eyes twinkled. "There was another book, too — one you will have never heard of in France — a German poem called *The Orphan Girl of the Pont des Arts.* I forgot who wrote it. Grillparzer, I fancy. Ask

Thomas — I expect he can recite it all from memory, even now. The *Pont des Arts*," he repeated, rubbing his knee with a quick, brisk gesture, in token of some inward satisfaction. "When you have a son who is always reading the same books — you look out. He'll be up to something, be sure of that. I was young, and I didn't understand at the time. Even when he said to me one day — I think he'd been having an argument with his sisters — 'Aren't I a bit French, Uncle Bela?' I laughed and said: 'Yes, just about as much as I'm Turkish. My great-great-grandmother came from Üsküb, so you see you're French and I'm Turkish.' He didn't laugh, or get angry, but just said: 'All the same, I *am* a bit French' — and went off again to his stove.

"All young male creatures get wild sometime over something. Even I — though I'm an old mummy these days — even I got wild over a woman more than once." He suddenly turned his profile towards me, and as he ran his fingers over the hair above his ear, I noticed a thin white line among the gray. "I went off the rails — deliberately, I daresay — however, I did. But Thomas, at any rate at that age, wasn't interested in women. What roused him was — " and he jerked his fat index finger in the direction of my chest — "you. You — the French people." His corpulent person again quaked with silent laughter. "Do you deserve such devotion? On one side of the Danube the answer would be, Yes; on the other side of it, No: according to the incidence of the Treaty of Trianon. However, that's what it was. He had fallen in love with the French nation. I used to laugh at him, and so did his mother. Even when he recited Hugo for our benefit, and I can assure you that when he got going it was something of a performance. But we just laughed.

"We laughed," he said once more, slowly lifting his heavy eyelids like some great pachyderm. And between the fat folds of flesh I caught a genial twinkle as he added:"And was it wholly regrettable?"

ๆๆ

What transformed Thomas's wild dreams into something resembling the germ of a decision was possibly a family conference that took place in the old Devîn house when he was getting on for sixteen. He heard his mother and his uncle settling his fate with unsuspecting callousness, while he, with his forehead against the window, watched the

Morava at the foot of the cliff heaving its green waters into the muddy billows of the Danube, the river Danube which thenceforward was to be the background of his life. Accursed Danube! Not that he didn't love the Danube. But why didn't it rise in France? If only he could have hoped sometimes to see barges or tugs flying the tri-color ensign, and coming from the wondrous West! No; never any flags but Austrian and German. And now and again a Rumanian one — with its ridiculous yellow stripe sandwiched between blue and red.

The death of his cousin Latzi brought matters to a head. Thomas did not like him, incidentally. Latzi's pride — he was a military cadet at Budapest — was only equaled by that of his father, a portentous Counselor of State, Szechenyi, Secretary of the Inland Transport Department. Anyone who wasn't a cadet was beneath notice. One day a fellow cadet jostled him in a doorway. Latzi insisted on an apology. Apology? To a Slovak? The other spat at his feet. Latzi recoiled, and flung his glove into the lad's face, which the latter did not deign to pick up. He went in quest of seconds, but none were forthcoming. Everyone declined, even the other Slovaks. Latzi, quite frantic by this time, was conscious of a sort of soft, unyielding opposition all around him:

he felt as though his feet were somehow caught and bogged, and he himself encompassed by a strange mystery of lowered eyes and constrained smiles. At last one of his fellows made up his mind to tell him what every lad in the school knew except himself, what had always been concealed from him by the imbecile vanity of his father, the Privy Councilor; and that was that his eminently pious mother, Cadet Ladislas Szechenyi's mother, was a Jewess. Cadet Szechenyi a Jewess's son! He, like his companions, looked upon Jews as something lower than mongrels; he would make a Jew give up his seat to him in a train. He was found, at the dawn of day, after a night of what must have been ghastly mental torment, hanged in his bedroom.

The whole story was told to Thomas, with a sort of whispered complacency, by his uncle's secretary. It made Thomas ill — physically ill. This was plain barbarism. Was he to pass his life, his whole life, in that senile country, among a pack of feathered savages, when over yonder — and not so very far away — lay a land of free men? France, radiant, generous, the domain of intellect and justice.

What followed might indeed be reduced to the dimensions of a sudden impulse. I think that would be a false rendering of the facts. In the first place because no act born of love is ever an act of impulse. Also, when a lad saves up his pennies month by month until he has enough to carry out his plan, what he does on the day he puts that plan into execution (even if he hadn't yet made up his mind the very day before) can scarcely be described as an impulse. And, in the event, when a whole life, a whole existence, pursued with wisdom, prudence, and resolve, follows rigorously from a given act, that act, ill-considered as it may appear, is more than likely to have been the outcome of a rational decision.

ം

That very night Thomas Muritz packed his knapsack. Dawn saw him on the road beyond the Danube leading to Vienna. Not the shortest road, but the more northerly one, through Wagram. It was a dream of his to sleep at Wagram.

He had not set out at random, not by any means. For months past he had planned out his route in all its stages, and his very modest budget. Travel by train was out of the question. He would sleep in barns (it was May and the weather was mild). He would do his marketing in the villages: a little bread, a scrap of meat, and some fruit. His whole object was to get to Troyes with a little money in his pocket; then, and not till then, he had made up his mind to take the train.

He was well prepared for the dust of the roads, the mist on the mountains, the exhaustion of the day's end; but though he had steeled himself against the rain, the wind, the noonday sun, bruised and bleeding feet, nights on the hard ground, sweat and thirst, he had no intention of arriving with wearied limbs at the precise point he had fixed upon as his journey's end. Hunger mattered nothing, but on that day he meant to be alert and fresh. For the goal of his journey was, above all, France; more precisely still, it was Paris; but still more so, it was that one place, unique and wonderful, that haunted his thoughts, nourished his dreams, and set his soul on fire: the *Pont des Arts.*

ల౬

I suppose this will provoke a smile or two. Fantastic, of course: he was sacrificing all that would make his life happy and contented, the warmth of home, an affectionate and beloved mother (he adored her all his life), a secure and easy future; he was facing a hazardous journey, with all its dangers and fatigues, all the trials that must follow upon migration into another country (for though he knew he would not starve, he quite realized that he would be in for a hard time) — and all this for a vision of the Pont des Arts! Ah well! those of you who have spent your day behind a more or less managerial desk, interviewing men whom you either mistrust or despise, contending, maneuvering and bluffing, fighting your hardest for a few thousand sordid francs, you may smile indeed. But I, my fat friend, do not smile. It is by such fantastications that I measure love. The passion of love does not move me to smiles: and least of all a boy's love.

Boyhood is terribly serious — don't forget that. A boy flings his whole being into his acts. And when are grave and reverend personages like ourselves prepared to do likewise? We attach too much importance to our cherished carcasses. This was very observable when those substantial citizens of ours, in their various uniforms, abandoned their beaten troops, and crammed their families and cashboxes into high-powered cars, and so sped to the other end of France. No, Thomas Muritz's far-off passion

for the Pont des Arts did not make me smile. My
heart went out to him when I heard the story. And
I hope, for my soul's sake, that it will never make
me smile.

∞

Yes, it is always with a stab of affection that I
picture that beloved shade on the dusty road,
making his way, dogged and intent, towards that
dazzling country to which he had given his alle-
giance. The loaded Tyrolean knapsack drags at his
shoulders, he cranes his neck forward, he swings
his clumsy hands as he plods along. When I knew
him first he was still young, and yet already rather
stocky, not able to stand great heat or long dis-
tances. Nothing in the world will induce me to
believe that he was ever a walker or an athlete. And
on that road I cannot picture him otherwise than a
weary figure, uncoiling, day upon day, the endless
chain of that stubborn martyrdom. Indeed he said
as much himself: "It was hard going," he used to
say, in that faintly halting utterance which found
expression in such odd abbreviations. "It was certainly hard going. But — Hugo!" And that name
made all things clear. For what sustained him in

that exhausting ordeal was exactly what sustained
the weary Crusaders: love, faith — and the saints.

But it was also the vision of the glories of Jeru-
salem. For Thomas, it was the lure of the city of
Paris, overflowing with humanity and history; those
stones and streets and purlieus that came to life in
the novels of Dumas, Balzac, and Eugène Sue.

❧

An intellectual love, you would suggest? Nonsense! Was there anything intellectual about the
love that brought those simple folk thronging to
the tomb of Christ? Such also is the love of France.
France is not an ordinary country, loved solely because a man has had the good fortune, deserved or
not, to be a man of France from one generation to
the next. The love of France is not the attachment
of the beast to its lair, or of the Teuton to his tribe.
In the love of France there is the Christian's faith
in his Redeemer. With those who do not understand I can but sympathize.

❧

Up to his arrival at the French frontier, I knew
very little of the story. Those weeks' laborious

journeying was no more than a monotonous memory in his mind. "Following a Star," he described it with a smile, adding that like the Wise Men of old he could look at nothing but the orb that guided him upon his way. "But what about the Tyrol?" I exclaimed, for I always felt that everyone must share my love of mountains. "Well," he said, "I walked through the Tyrol and I found it as tiring to walk downhill as I did to walk uphill." Which was all he had to say about the Tyrol. Still, I couldn't help being rather taken aback. "The point was to get here," he said, trying to make himself clear. "If you start admiring things, you have to stop. Every delay meant a risk to the delights ahead of me" — a smile flashed across his short, trimmed beard: "I had to . . . I had to reach France with enough money in my pocket; I wanted — don't laugh! — I wanted to sleep, my first night in France, in a bed, a French bed."

This he achieved — for indeed he always managed to achieve the tasks imposed on him by the passion that was his. He crossed the frontier at Delle on Midsummer Day. He changed what money remained to him and reckoned up his resources: forty-odd francs. All was well. Three francs for a square meal — the first one! — and a night in an inn; so much he had promised himself. Thenceforward he continued on his frugal way. His intention was to live on two francs a day. He would take the train at Troyes; that also was a promise to himself. Even so he would arrive in the possession of more than twelve francs: he would have time to turn round.

God shields a lover and rewards an ardent heart. Some notice nothing, and take what comes to them for granted; others, on the contrary, express their ardor by exulting in everything as a wonderful experience, always at the height of their expectation. Thomas was of this kind: he passed the day in ecstasy. The lovely weather, the smooth and easy road, the fresh green of the trees and meadows, all seemed in his eyes the entrancing presage of a splendid welcome — the sort of welcome that he looked to find in France. He was delighted to learn that the river, on the bank of which stood the inn where he stopped, just as the sun was sinking behind the tall poplars, was called "La Savoureuse." He was delighted with the inn, and the omelette (his first encounter with French cooking!) placed before him, a twelve-egged omelette, all of which he ate voraciously, under the somewhat wondering gaze of the innkeeper, who, however, made no remark, though he was contemplating the disappearance of what was intended for the family dinner. And when Thomas understood what had happened, he was delighted with the innkeeper. He was still more delighted with him a little later on, and indeed his meeting with the man was to remain an imperishable memory for the rest of his life. "He stands to me as a symbol," he would say. "When I think of the Czechs, it is always my Uncle Karel that I see before me, with his blond mustachios curling into side whiskers. Which is foolish, I know, for it was much less Czech than Austrian. And when I think of the French, it is that face I see, the rather drawn face of my excellent russet-haired innkeeper. The long, pink nose, and the reddish straggling mustache which he used to draw into his mouth with a spongy sort of smack after drinking. And, above all, those blue eyes, dreamy yet intent — the quiet eyes of a free human being, trained to use and listen to reason." The innkeeper came up. He smiled, and little fans of wrinkles spread out over his temples.

"Feeling better?" said he. "You were hungry, eh?"

Thomas was not taken aback by the man's

familiar address. And he answered, with grave cordiality:

"Yes, citizen."

This time the ginger mustache lifted to reveal an array of pointed white teeth.

"You're from Austria?" he asked.

"From Moravia," said Thomas with precision.

"Are you in France for long?"

"For ever."

The man grinned through the comblike partings in his mustache. Then he said:

"I suppose you have no family alive."

"Indeed I have," said Thomas. "There's my mother, and my sisters — and my uncle, the ship-owner. That's just it."

"Just what?"

"Well, I should have spent all my life at Pressburg."

A shadow like a sudden cloud darkened the innkeeper's face.

"You've run away from home?"

"France is a free country, citizen."

The mustache had ceased to smile, and the blue eyes were fixed upon him with a strange and rather disquieting gaze. Ah, thought Thomas, this is the dangerous moment. And he saw himself handed over to the police, put onto a train, and returned to his family.

But, suddenly:

"By God," cried the innkeeper, "you're right. Yes, France is a free country. Mariette!"

A shadowy form emerged from a deeper shadow: a form habited entirely in black. Neither young, nor beautiful. But the expression of the face was clear and serene.

"Look at this lad," said her husband. "He comes from the Danube. He has left everything behind him there — his mother, and everything he has. And do you know why? Because France is a free country."

"And of course you have congratulated him on doing so," said the woman quietly. "Please listen to me," she said to Thomas. "You go back home."

"Ah!" exclaimed her husband. "Now she's off! Just you listen to her, my young friend."

"A free country? It's rather too soon to say so. Ten years! Freedom is still quite a new toy for him and his like," and she jerked her head at the innkeeper.

"Mariette!" bellowed her husband.

"A toy — which they will break, or wear out, or

get sick of. Don't you have anything to do with it. It's quite risky enough for the people of this country. I hate to think he dragged my little girl off to see the tree of liberty planted! My little Titine, not yet six years old."

"She'll never forget that as long as she lives," said the man.

"It's dreadful to see them making all this fuss and flourish about Liberty, without realizing that they're being watched from every side. Wait till they go just a little too far, and they'll soon see what's coming to them. Take care not to be here when that happens, my young friend."

"You hear what she says," said the man, getting up. "That is the voice of prudence. And now listen to mine. But first I must say a word she did not utter. The word is — justice. That's what she has forgotten. . . ."

"I didn't forget anything," said the woman, receding into the shadow. "Poor little lad; justice, indeed!"

". . . That," he went on, "is what she has forgotten — and justice comes before liberty. What's the good of liberty if not to help us to be just? Never you mind the old lady. She's a grand soul; but she's nervous because she has seen some rough doings in her time. I've seen just as much, and I daresay I should be just as nervous, if it wasn't for my faith in justice. Which is why a man has no right to be nervous. Besides, we must always remember that this isn't a woman's business at all. It's our business: a matter between men. And I'm free to tell you that you have done well to come, because, as I see it, justice is what we are most set on in this country. It's my notion that France is the soldier of justice, as you might say. We are her soldiers. There can never be too many of them. And if you have come here to join us, why, you'll be very welcome."

"I have certainly come to join you," said Thomas, and a thrill of exultation filled his eyes with tears.

"Then, from today, you are one of us," said the landlord gravely, putting his arm round the lad's shoulders. "And if you are ever in trouble one of these days, remember me."

က

"You are one of us." Those were the words used by the first Frenchman who had spoken to him. If, in fact, Thomas's youth hadn't blinded him to

the touch of undue unction in the landlord's ob-
servations, he would have refused to admit it, for
the sake of those very words. As for myself, well,
I'm not ashamed to admit that a certain grandiloquence can rouse me when it comes from a sincere and simple heart. I like that landlord. As for
Thomas, he didn't need to be in trouble, I fancy,
before remembering him; indeed, he never forgot
him all his life long. But when the day came, when
I must needs believe, alas, that it was this never-
forgotten face, that "little red-haired fellow's" face,
that Thomas saw before him in his hour of death,
it is I who am troubled — and ashamed.

ᦂ

The Troyes train pulled into the station late in
the evening. The sun was already low on the
horizon, the houses plunged in shadow save for the
topmost stories which gleamed in a sunset splendor
of gold and pink. Thomas Muritz lost no time. He
was hungry, and his knapsack had grown very
heavy. Should he look for a restaurant, or a hotel?
No: the sun would not wait. Resolutely he made
his way along the Boulevard de Strasbourg (he
knew the map of Paris by heart), turned down the

Boulevard Sébastopol, then into the Rue de Tur-
bigo, the Central Market, and the Rue du Louvre.
And, just as the sun was setting, he came at last to
the goal of his journey — to the place of all places,
the vision of which had sustained him all the way
from Pressburg, through the dust of the roads, the
chill of the valleys, the tempests on the peaks, and
the never-ending torment of his stiffened limbs —
to the very embodiment of all the presentations
of his passion: the Pont des Arts. He was there —
he was positively there! And his expectation was
indeed fulfilled. He had not been deceived: nor,
mark you, had his passion deceived him either. He
had been guided straight to the heart of his aspira-
tions, to that point upon the globe where, with
scarce a movement, he who stands can see around
him the Institut, the Louvre, the Cité — and the
Bookstall quays, the Tuileries, the Latin Hill as
far as the Panthéon, the Seine up to the Concorde.
A panorama that filled his heart with an ecstasy
almost too tremendous to be borne. He stood there,
while the last rays of the sun shimmered behind
Passy, flooded the spire of Notre-Dame with ver-
milion, and flickered on the pinnacles and turrets
of the Louvre. Under his feet flowed, proud and
aloof, a river that had no need, like the Danube or

the Ultava, to attract remark in order to be admired. At that hour its waters slid past, luminous
and heavy, like iridescent quicksilver. Barges
drifted by. Artists on the banks were packing up
to go home. Fishermen placidly fished on. Students
and old gentlemen lingered on the quays and
rummaged in the book boxes. Lively little shop-
girls passed and looked with eyes of curiosity and
wonder at this ingenuous youth so lost in impassive
contemplation, who gave them no responding look.

At this point I fear I shall have to put in a word.
I ought, it would seem, to make clear that I am not
telling the story of an imaginary character, but of a
man, compounded of flesh and blood. The rights
and obligations of a novelist and of a biographer
are not identical. There are, in particular, chances
and coincidences which a novelist may not use,
since he is their master, and would thus lay himself
open to the charge of disloyalty to his art. Even a
biographer is often tempted to leave them aside,
for improbability makes him uncomfortable. All
of which considered, I should probably have not
mentioned what then happened on the Pont des
Arts, if, in the accounts of Thomas's pilgrimage
that I got from his wife, his son, and his friends,
and on which the present narrative is based — if the

encounter which befell Thomas on that bridge had not been as strange in its utter unexpectedness as in its effect on Thomas Muritz. Indeed, I don't think there could be any incident in which Thomas's consuming passion seems more natural and vivid — or more appealing, I might add. There he was, right in the middle of the Pont des Arts, "stiff and motionless, like one of the ancient kings on the Old Bridge in Prague" — so said, many years later, the man who met him there. The man's name was Gallerand. He was the foreign representative of the Rhône-Danube Company. Thomas remembered having often seen him in his father's and his uncle's houses. He was, in absolute fact, the only human being whom he knew in Paris. "Gallerand will help me," he had thought more than once while on the road. How was he to find him? He did not know, but that did not worry him much. And here was this very man, the improbable Gallerand, who had stopped ten feet away and was now eying him. An unimaginable chance? Of course; but when I consider the immense part that chance does play, and how often the course of so humdrum a life as mine has turned on chance, I am scarcely surprised at one chance the more. I feel much more inclined to be surprised at Thomas

Muritz's behavior on that occasion: which was indeed what Gallerand used to be surprised at when he told the story. "Do you think he was astonished?" said he. "There was good reason to be astonished, wasn't there? I waited — and I smiled, as I waited to see him start, or cry out, or something. Not a bit of it. When he turned and caught sight of me, he smiled and said quietly, 'Good morning, M. Gallerand,' and took off his hat exactly as if we had met in Market Street at Pressburg. And when I had made him tell the whole story, and learned that here he was, at sunset, in a strange city, without relatives, friends, lodging, or work, and without money, except for the two five-franc pieces he showed me, and when I said: 'My poor lad, what on earth is all this? What would have become of you? Do you realize that if you hadn't met me . . .?'

" 'But I was sure I should meet you,' said he, and for the first time he showed signs of surprise."

He was indeed surprised. And what surprised him was Gallerand's surprise. For, after all, what was there very surprising in such a meeting on the Pont des Arts? Where, indeed, would one be likely to meet if not on the Pont des Arts? Could anyone live in Paris and not make a point of crossing the

31

Pont des Arts as often as he could? Such was the
force of the passion that possessed him. And such
was its endurance that he was still a little surprised
forty years later: even then, that was the place
where anyone who wanted to meet Thomas Muritz
would have been pretty sure to do so, at any season
of the year, without more trouble than a little
assiduity.

∽

Gallerand took him home. He asked him what
he meant to do, whether he had any sort of plan in
his mind. Well, of course Thomas had a plan.
Indeed, he had but one plan, one sole aim that he
wanted to achieve, of which the Pont des Arts was
only the first stage. His purpose centered on the
works of Balzac, Hugo, and Eugène Sue, those
entrancing volumes which had been as bread and
wine to him, the intoxicating draught which had
thrilled him into the discovery of his own self,
those odes to Paris, to France and her people, to
love and justice, those dazzling and familiar pages;
he meant somehow to make them known in the
humblest households of their native land. And
he succeeded. I have already said that he always

succeeded in every demand imposed on him by his inspiring passion. He asked Gallerand to help him to get a job in a bookseller's shop. And this was done without very much trouble. He first ran errands, then tied up the parcels, and then was put on to stocktaking. He left that modest establishment for a more important man of books, a publisher, where he was soon in charge of the mail-order department. Later on he applied to represent the firm in the provinces as their traveling agent. And when he judged himself sufficiently well up in the trade, and had laboriously accumulated enough capital to make the venture, he founded the Muritz editions. Today they are forgotten. They had but an ephemeral life, under that name at least — indeed, they lasted only a few years. Thus the butterfly, after a long life spent in the chrysalis, emerges for the sole purpose of laying eggs, and dies. In the same way, Thomas Muritz founded his house solely to establish, as the result of his experience, a system which enabled him to introduce into many, many thousand homes, in the form of Sunday *feuilletons*, those works he so adored — Balzac, Hugo, and Eugène Sue. That achieved, he lost interest in his business and sold it.

Such is the force of passion, but it is a jealous and devouring element, and therefore to be dreaded. Within the mind of him that harbors it nothing but that fixed idea can live. It makes a holocaust of impulses and concepts, on which indeed it gluts its greedy, cancerous life. And when, by good or evil fortune, it does disappear, satiated or self-consumed, it leaves a ghastly emptiness behind it, and the soul of its possessor stripped of all desires — except the craving for a renewal of that servitude.

Fortunately for Thomas Muritz, he was not immediately aware of the void within him left by the achievement of his task — which was doubtless what saved him from those disastrous consequences. The fact was that his passion had two aspects: Paris, and the authors who had revealed her secret. When he had paid them the homage on which he had spent those fifteen years, and found himself still seething with forces which he no longer knew how to control, he could at least still rejoice in his love for the great city; and so he did with all the ardor he had lavished on honoring her poets. Not a street, not an alley, that did not one day see him pass. Did he dream, in the course of that slow and passionate possession, of marking the imprint of his

passage on the city of his devotion? If he did, he
succeeded. He made a new street, and built the
houses either side of it.

He was never wearied or weakened by his passion. Aloof and intense it always was. What a misery he looked when dragged away by his family
to take a holiday in the mountains or by the sea!
Haggard and bent, afraid of the heat and the cold,
the sun and wind and rain, and of boredom above
all, he counted the days until he could get back
to his beloved Paris! Away from that cherished
city he could enjoy nothing. He exclaimed against
any sort of hot weather in the country, though the
moment he got back he was very ready to risk a
sunstroke by crossing the blazing Place du Car-
rousel in the noontide heat. How he hated the Al-
pine mists; and how he dreamed of the Rue des
Sts.-Pères, gleaming under the chill rains of Oc-
tober, and longed to be walking down it, peering
into the antique shops. The spectacle of the heaving ocean merely filled him with boredom and
disgust: he craved the cafés of the Boulevard
St.-Michel where he would sit for hours contemplating the youth of many nations interminably
flowing by.

He had become a Frenchman. I can still see him

on the day when my father told him the great news. It was outside some café, near the Ministry of the Interior. I still carry the vision of that sunny day, the dusty highway, and the municipal water cart. I can still see his expression, his smile that strove to mask its apprehension as we came up. I was then a small boy. I remember they drank a glass of absinthe together, and how my rare and precious pleasure in sitting outside a café was thereby spoilt, for I had lately seen an antialcoholic propaganda film, and was afraid that my father and Thomas would, promptly, and under my very eyes, go mad. Horror-struck, I watched them drain their glasses. I searched the drinkers' faces for the dreadful symptoms. But the face of Thomas Muritz depicted nothing but an immensity of joy. "I am French," he muttered, and he looked about him with an air of surprise as though the scene had somehow changed since the marvelous announcement. I also was surprised, for I could then see nothing extraordinary in being French. Now, hardly a day passes that I do not tell myself, as did Thomas Muritz, that it is indeed a far from ordinary matter.

He had married. And even his marriage was a stanza in that long canticle to France. This time I say France, and not Paris. The typical Paris woman attracted him, but he would never have met with one he wanted to marry. What he looked for in a wife were the homely sort of virtues: above all, she must spring from the ancient soil of France, and her children and his must be firmly rooted in that soil.

In that, too, he succeeded. The owner of the restaurant where he dined had a niece; she came to Paris to spend her holidays with her uncle, and the deities of love and chance conspired to put him in her way. She proved the incarnation of his dream: pretty, modest, cheerful, candid, sentimental, and virtuous — and her name was Chambord. She was, like Eugénie Grandet, the daughter of a cooper, who had, however, not made money. She was twenty years old, and taught in the little local school in her native village of Vendoeuvres, in the Berry country.

Pretty, virtuous, and such a name — Chambord! She promptly took to Thomas; she liked him for his delicate features and convincingly male beard, his air of quiet distinction, the prudence and self-mastery that controlled a really venturesome and romantic temperament; though her notion of where Moravia might be, Thomas's native land, was very vague.

I wish I could tell you the story of that marriage. It was a charming and affectionate courtship. Their betrothal took place during the Christmas holidays — she confiding and a little bewildered, he, for once, shy and nervous. Then they parted until the summer; it was his decision, but he found that parting very hard to bear. In those days, whenever he could get away, he would mount his motor tricycle (then the latest novelty), dash through the Porte d'Orléans, and speed for ten or twenty kilometers in the direction of Vendoeuvres, where he pictured the girl surrounded by her inky-fingered little charges, and then, relieved at having approached a little nearer to her, come home again. It is to be remembered that he had already reached the age and station in life when respectable citizens usually devote their blandishments to Boards of Directors.

I wish I could tell you about the ceremony itself: the wedding breakfast, at the farm of the bride's foster-father; the guests who first sang, turn by turn, the rustic, rough old catches that belong to such occasions, and then gradually broke into the chants of the countryside, lamentations over the sufferings of the poor, the greed and tyranny of the rich. . . . "Bless them all," said Thomas to himself, and while the company embraced him, teased him, and slapped him on the back, his recollection sped back to the innkeeper on the banks of the Savoureuse, the worthy little redheaded fellow who had said: "You are one of us."

II. THE REIGN OF GREED

It is not enough to possess the Sun if we know
not how to make his light shine upon others.
— PAUL CLAUDEL, *Saint Louis*

∾

To ANDRÉ, who died for France:
And to his brother GEORGES, wounded in
the service of France:
To MAX, who died for France,
To LUCIEN who died for France.

To ROBERT and to RAYMOND,
To HENRI, MAURICE, and HENRY,
To BENJAMIN, JEAN-RICHARD, and PIERRE,
To RAYMOND and RUDI —
who fought in both wars.

To ÉTIENNE, who fought in Libya.

And to all those who are not, like them,
My friends, and brothers.

> You had never wounded me so sorely
> had you not, having wounded me, departed.
> — PAUL CLAUDEL, *Saint Louis*

A S I SAID, he expected from his marriage
children who should be soundly rooted in the ancient soil of France. His son, indeed, is so deeply
embedded in that soil that he has sunk beyond
our vision.

André, beloved playmate of my boyhood, has
slept for twenty-five years in the cold earth, engulfed by the fatal shell that blew up his battery;
but he has never faded from my memory. Who
could forget his radiant face? His boyish charm,
his gaiety, his enthusiasm, and his sparkling intelligence. My father enjoyed teasing him, for the
pleasure of hearing his retorts. He was so fond of
all André's little ways, his perfervid patriotism, and
his comically pious resolve never to touch anything
that could bring Germany to mind; even to the
point, once, of refusing a pudding because it was
described as *Bavaroise* on the hotel menu. One day,
I remember, he was caught out; he was eagerly

lapping up a plate of *St.-Germain* soup. "I'm doing it on purpose," he retorted with a laugh. "Just to show the Boches how we'll swallow them up one day."

Do you remember, André — ah, I talk as if you were still with us — those last holidays, in 1914, in that little village at the head of a dark Swiss valley? There it was that war surprised us, and surprised your father most of all. He was overwhelmed. Not that he was afraid for your sake, or for his own: you were so young, and he was already too old. He was afraid for France — for the land of France, and for her people. All night his teeth chattered, and his bed shook. He, alone perhaps among us all, did indeed envisage all the horrors that threatened those he loved so well.

We parted with a laugh. You whispered in my ear: "As soon as I'm through my exams, I shall join up." And Thomas let you do it. Indeed, how could he have prevented you? It was he himself who had bred in you that fervid love for France.

Just as legend molds the form of heroes into the semblance of something truer than nature, so my vision of you now is perhaps much more akin to that delightful caricature by one of our friends at Fontainebleau than to your face as it was in life.

It was so like you, and you were so popular, that it was reproduced on a postcard. It depicted you, dashing, gay, and gallant, in your uniform, handsome as Louis XV in boyhood, stepping out of an eggshell, with the legend: "Spring Chicken, the youngest officer in France." It was not long before you were the youngest of her dead.

I detest the sort of father who boasts of "having given his sons to France." Few men, in my view, are more deserving of contempt than old Doumer, who hoisted himself into public estimation by the aid of four sons killed. Indeed, I would not have mentioned his sacrifice at all, if it were solely to win sympathy for Thomas Muritz. But the father's grief went far beyond the patriot's pride. And of that grief I remember only this, that it banished once for all his fear that he might not be judged as French as any of his fellows.

More than once, at dinners, receptions, bridge parties, some ill-mannered oaf had, in his presence, made contemptuous reference to "imported Frenchmen." Out of regard for his hosts, Thomas denied himself the relief of retaliation by challenging the man to produce anything more to his credit than the accident of having been born here rather than elsewhere, in comparison with what he, Thomas

Muritz, had done to prove his devotion to the country he had chosen for his own. Could he, as could Thomas, say to France, like Claudel's Saint Louis:

> Is it my body only that you ask of me — is it not my soul?
> Surely your power upon my heart reaches beyond all material things,
> Stands where time stands no longer, and separation can no longer be.
> That which was solely appetite has passed into thought, decision, honour, loyalty, and acceptance self-imposed.
> The kiss while the spirit sleeps now passes into longing, never to be satisfied,
> For a paradise remote and unachieved, where every living being may find inspiration.
> My love is no chance love, but born of justice and necessity. . . .

"My love for you is no chance love, but born of justice and necessity." He never said anything though he was angry with himself for saying nothing, and was as much vexed by his own silence as by what the other man had said. "Fortunately," he said, in his quiet voice, and with that trick he had of leaving out his verbs: "fortunately always the same sort of fellow . . . neat and smart and smug, with meticulously parted hair. Never, thank heaven, one of my grand little redheaded friends." For he spoke of them in the plural, as though all the best people in that beloved country must needs have red hair. I mentioned this to him on one occasion. I knew about the innkeeper, of course; but —

"There were others," he said. "Redheaded men have always brought me luck. Well, I don't know — I often feel as though the genius of France had sent me, half in humor, all those amusing little fellows as her emissaries: the emissaries of what is finest in this people. I shall never forget the red-haired fellow in the omnibus, the night of Ferrer's death. (You remember Ferrer?) Quite a young fellow, that one was — "

"O yes, Ferrer — I believe I've read his story. But I don't remember it very well. And who was your redheaded fellow?"

I liked to make him talk. It was difficult to get him to start. He so rarely brought himself to utter more than a few words, and when he did, they were well worth the hearing.

"Read *The White Wine of La Villette*," said he. "It's very well and convincingly written. Just the account of the trial, which was sickening enough. But they shot him! Imagine shooting a man for his

47

ideals! Yes, I know it all happened in Spain; but when I read it in the newspaper, I fairly jumped. I was on the platform at Auteuil-St.-Sulpice, I remember."

"You mean the old rattletrap tramway — with an extra horse to help it uphill?"

"Yes, do you remember it?"

"But tell me about the red-haired fellow."

"He was a little plumber, who peered over my arm at the paper. Red-haired, as I've told you. I don't say he was much like my innkeeper. Still — he had the same sort of wrinkled face, and a long tawny mustache. . . . He read the headlines, gasped, and looked at me. Which was odd, because at that time I prided myself on being well dressed. I wore a gray bowler and spats, so I couldn't have looked the sort of person to whom he would feel drawn. Perhaps it was because he saw me start. Or perhaps he just couldn't help exchanging a look with someone. At any rate he looked at me, I looked at him, we both of us wagged our heads, and went on doing so for a moment or two, I expect because we could neither of us think of anything to say; when I remember the scene today, I feel we must have seemed rather a comical pair. But we didn't feel like laughing."

"Didn't you say anything at all?"

"Yes — at last he said: 'When did they kill him?' "

" 'Yesterday morning.'

" 'The swine,' he said, whistling through his teeth. Then he set his jaw, and began to wag his head again. It was quite enough to indicate what was in his mind. And indeed it soothed me to feel I wasn't alone in my wrath. I daresay he felt the same. In any case he suddenly gripped my arm and said in a harsh, tense voice:

" 'I must go and see the lads.'

"He got off, and without thinking I got off when he did. It was by the Place St.-Charles. We started to walk. And we talked — how we talked! Then we turned into a bar. It was empty. People often say hard things about bars, but, finding it empty, I understood that a bar can be a comfort, on occasions. The landlord said: 'Try Albert's place.' And we set out again. We turned under an archway, and at the far end of a yard my redheaded friend ushered me into a sort of workshop in which stood rows of large and rather dusty tables littered with parcels. There were already half a dozen fellows in the room. My companion did not introduce me, and I was eyed with a certain amount of curiosity, but we were all so excited that two minutes afterwards some of them were already treating me like an old acquaintance. Others entered. My little red-haired friend was heard with much attention. He often turned towards me to appeal for my support, and we all stared into each other's eyes. I don't know how long we stayed there. Some went out, others came in, and every time the same words were spoken, just as one prods at a sore gum. In the end, of course, we had to part. But it was agreed that we should meet again. And when we did, our feelings had in no way cooled. My new friend promptly stood beside me, as though he and I had been the inspirers of all this indignation. And there we were, all talking again — we couldn't help prodding that sore gum. We didn't quite know what we were waiting for, if indeed we were waiting for anything. In the end a tall fellow came in, a dashing lad with a very Gallic mustache — and a red one, mark you! — shouting: 'They're going to the Embassy,' upon which he promptly turned and went out again. I didn't know who 'they' might be, but I well understood which Embassy was meant. We all went out. My little redheaded friend kept close at my side: and indeed I was glad to have him with me. As we turned into the Boulevard de Grenelle we made out other groups in the dusk moving towards the Champ de Mars; groups of three or four, and sometimes a dozen or more, like ourselves, emerging from every side street. We crossed the Seine. By the time we had reached the Champs-Élysées something like a crowd had gathered. It was humming like a hive of bees, which produced a strangely dizzying effect: I felt as though Paris were heaving beneath my feet. The Boulevard Haussmann was already packed, so that we could barely move; then a shout or two was heard. We too began to shout. We were never able to get near the Embassy, but we fairly shouted ourselves hoarse, in our anger, loathing, and despair. . . . I don't know why I tell you all this. I rather think I enjoy the recollection of it. . . . I feel — is it an awful thing to say? — I rather feel that I was never again so happy as I was that evening."

᪗

As for myself, nothing saddens me more than to recall his story of that evening: that noble burst of wrath, that grand uprush of the French conscience, over one man unjustly put to death. What, alas! would happen if there were occasion for such a demonstration these days? Ah, there could be no better indication of all that has been lost, of the degradation into which we were betrayed.

And now that I come to the bitterest page of all, I am only too conscious of that falling-off.

The Armistice found me, like many others, in the so-called free zone. I came back sooner than most. But even so I avoided Paris: the vision of that humiliated city, the difficulty of getting about, and all manner of harassments, trivial some of them but nonetheless paralyzing, kept me prisoner in a house that was for many weeks occupied by the military, and gradually stripped of its belongings. For many months I was without news of many friends. I wrote to Thomas Muritz, but got no reply. Indeed, I was not more concerned about him than about many others. The apathy, the self-imposed indifference of those days, was not the least of what we had to endure, for it was a defilement of our better selves.

When trains began to run again, I resumed my visits to Paris, though they were few and far between. I seldom spent more than forty-eight hours in the capital. I lacked the courage to face those various symbols of disgrace — the flags, the placards, the newspapers, and — later on — the stars on the garments of the Jews.

I saw one of them approaching me on a clear morning in June. I blushed, as I always did, for never once was I able to encounter one without blushing. And I had already begun to turn away my head with that wretched cowardice that always prevented me from conveying in a look the brotherly greeting that could alone have eased my shame; despite myself, my gaze was sinking towards the pavement when I glimpsed a short snow-white beard, a high clear forehead, and a smiling look, so full of sweetness, which I surely recognized.

But I was puzzled by that star. And my shocked memory flashed before me all I knew of Thomas Muritz's family — his ancestors, Calvinists every one of them.

Suddenly, too, I envisaged him, in days long past, marching indomitably towards the high-hearted land of France. God in Heaven, was it really all to end in this — the Star of Jewry?

He took my arm, and inquiring affectionately after me and my relations led me gently towards the steps down to the little square by the riverside, by the Seine quay, which looks towards both the Cité and the Île St.-Louis. But I could only mumble a few words in reply, as I struggled to recover from the conflicting emotions at finding him thus, an impressive if rather emaciated old gentleman, but still like himself, and at seeing him, of all men, wearing that emblem. As I went on mumbling, he pressed my arm affectionately to indicate he wanted to sit down. Then he smiled, and there was no hint of bitterness in that smile.

"Was it you," said he, "or was it André, who told me about an old mathematics master's remark about Cambronne's favorite term of abuse? 'It doesn't hurt anyone,' he said; 'it merely defiles the lips of him who uses it.' "

"Exactly," I exclaimed. "That's just why I feel . . ."

"You should not worry. Let the conqueror defile himself: it is all to the good of France."

"But that's just what France — and *we*, and *I* are doing. . . ."

"Well — and what then? Would you stand up to tanks unarmed? Or wear a star yourself like all those young students who are now slowly perishing in prison?"

"But why on earth are *you* wearing it?" I cried. "Surely — "

"After all, a Calvinist can quite well be a Jew. Up to what point, I don't know, and indeed I don't want to know. My mother was a Jew. As for my

father — all the male line were Calvinists. On the
female side, there were, I know, some more Jews.
How many, and who they were — well, Moravia is
too far off to find out now: besides, it's little I care,
my boy."

"I don't understand you, I don't understand
you," I cried (and it was true). "Some pure Jews
don't wear it, and I think they are quite right. And
you, who have every possible reason — "

"Oh, I'm too old, my boy."

There was silence for a moment, for I did not
at once grasp what he meant. Too old for what?
Not to wear the star? What had that got to do with
age?

"Well, you can't see me at my age," he went on,
"blowing up trains, or smuggling arms, or anything like that, can you? Nor, I suppose, do you
see me sitting placidly in my armchair — "

"You mean — "

"Yes: we must all serve the cause, in one way
or another. When men are persecuted, how shall
you recognize a Frenchman? And when France
herself is in agony, how shall you recognize her
sons? We may, indeed, preserve our own insignifi-
cant persons; but surely we must serve France in
doing so. And so, if we have no strength in us, let

us stay where we belong, among our own kind, and with them bear their cross."

"But when the sacrifice is vain — as yours is. When it is absolutely futile?"

"No sacrifice ever is so, and you know it. Are you one of those who accuse France of having flung herself into a conflict that was lost before it started? Of having leapt into the flames? Are you so blinded by all that is inevitably sordid and foul in a defeat that you cannot see that she will emerge from it greater than she was before?"

"I don't know," I said bluntly. "I wish I could be sure. She has indeed gone down into the mire. I'm afraid — I'm very much afraid that she will long bear the marks of it in men's memories."

"Of what? Defeat and rout and devastation?"

"Oh no; all that will be forgotten. Squalid it all was, and sad, but it will soon be no more than a tale that is told. It's the kind of thing that goes with every military disaster. No, I'm thinking of the shame that cannot be effaced. The badge you're wearing now. Our betrayal of the Lorrainers. And" — here I lowered my voice — "the degrading surrender of the political refugees — "

"What?"

As he uttered the word, it wasn't an exclama-

tion, nor even a cry: it was a kind of bark. I turned
to him, astonished. He was flushed, and his eyes
were bulging slightly. I recognized one of those
accesses of wrath that used to terrify his son.

"What's that you're saying? How dare you — "
He struck the pavement with his stick. "That filthy
lie!"

I said no more; and my surprise was so obvious
that it seemed to calm him down a little.

"Are you a fool, or worse? How can you demean
yourself to repeat one of the vilest slanders . . ."

"But, Monsieur Muritz — "

"Whose game do you think you're playing?
Don't you understand, my poor friend — it's German propaganda . . . they hope, by accusing us
of such an atrocity — "

"But, Monsieur Muritz, it's true! Alas, it's too
horribly true!"

I was getting rather heated myself, and I must
admit that I have never been so slow in the up-
take. Dear Thomas Muritz! To think that I failed
to understand you at that moment. I still cannot
think of it without a shudder.

He eyed me, all his anger fled, with no more than
that sort of impatient look we put on when scolding
an obstinate child.

"No, my young friend, it's not true. It most certainly is not true. It *can't* be true. Now listen."

He tapped my knee.

"Look here, my young friend. I don't like Pétain. God knows I don't. But all the same — now come! A Marshal of France. Surely now, a MARSHAL OF FRANCE."

Blessed Thomas, beloved Thomas, how innocent a heart was yours. Such is the power of history, and the words that are part of history, upon an ardent mind! A Marshal of France. And I began to think that my dear old friend must be right after all. It couldn't be true.

"So you really think — ?"

Alas, the words were well intended, but too promptly uttered. . . . Here again I blundered. I should not have changed my ground so quickly.

"Surely now," Thomas repeated, bending a little forward, "surely . . ."

He drew a few circles on the sand with the point of his stick. I racked my brains for something immediate to say, but without success, and the silence lasted just too long.

Then Thomas spoke at last, in faltering, hesitant tones —

"Because . . ." he said, and he dwelt heavily on

that one word, "because — if I were ever compelled to believe . . . if I found I could no longer . . ."

There he stopped. He had raised his head, and was looking across the Island, and the quay, to the houses ranging up the great hill of Ste.-Geneviève, and the dome that crowns them all, beneath which sleep so many famous men, and around which are gathered the Schools, and Colleges, and Faculties.

∾

That dome, and the mighty structure that supports it, filled the whole window of Stani's office. The sight of it quite weighed me down — and so did the force of Stani's personality and mind. Saints are not comfortable people to know. They hold up such a humiliating mirror to the common man, whose vanity is wounded by too much goodness.

I had climbed the stairs up to the third story, with a heart as heavy as the sky of that late autumn day. Of what would be said, I knew all I needed to know. More light could only bring more horror into view. But the light, though it be merciless, must be endured.

Stani opened the door himself. He was only at

home for a few days, until he could be provided with a safer refuge; nor was he sleeping in that house.

We had just got him out of his jail (I hesitate to include myself, because I played but little part in his deliverance, having done no more than arrange a few contacts among the right people). Everything was in order: papers, birth certificate — and none of them faked. Particular care was needed, for some enemy had denounced him as a Polish Jew — nor could we ever discover who had done so.

An enemy of Stani! It was hard to believe in one. True, saintliness and nobility of mind provoke as much hatred as do wealth and good fortune. Oh, the vileness of mankind!

Who was the viler: he who denounced him, or the official who delivered him to the enemy? "Fifty hostages tomorrow morning?" Certainly. And who should they be? Why, naturalized Jews, of course. An excellent idea! And so this great and good man was given up. His naturalization had been granted at the request of his admiring teachers, so that he could work in the laboratories in the Rue d'Ulm, where is evolved that omnipotent vaccine that saves so many thousands of French lives. He had, at his own wish, served through both wars in the ranks, and served to such purpose that he ended the first with several decorations, and the second with the loss of half an arm.

"You need not trouble," was the reply when, at Drancy, he asked for time to pack a suitcase. Thereby he knew his fate.

"I rather think I owe my life to an excess of zeal," he said. "They returned a hundred and fifty names, for fear that the fifty would not be produced in time. Well, their calculations worked out well enough, if rather on the generous side. There were a hundred of us herded in that horrible yard. . . . It was also lucky for me that the Fritzes didn't have the whole bunch of us shot, as they had us all there. However, a selection had to be made. Do you know how they made it?"

I shook my head. He had put me in one of those deep chairs which are called, I believe, club chairs, and as I lounged back in it, the warm room, the rugs and books and pictures, made his story seem hideously vivid, as well as fantastically unreal.

He paced slowly up and down, with a weary air, while I admired, as always, that noble head of his: it was the face of a John the Baptist, and its drawn features and deep-set lines could not mask its sweetness.

"I would rather," said he, "have been in my place than in theirs. French gendarmes! Ah well, I suppose we should pity the poor devils."

"Not on your life," I exclaimed. "They were cowards to a man."

Stani looked back at me over his shoulder, and smiled a melancholy smile. Then he closed his eyes and shrugged his shoulders.

"Pah!" said he. "They had their orders. Their lifelong training had been to find honor in obedience. Well, then — what constitutes the crime? At what stage does it begin, and where does it end? As for those poor brutes, I can just picture their dismay. Fifty only — and there were more than a hundred of us. A very awkward situation for them, and there was no time, you see, to get instructions. Indeed, I rather wonder whether it wasn't a little bit of extra sadism on Fritz's part, to force French gendarmes to choose the victims. . . ."

"I think it was to show their contempt, Stani."

"I daresay. But contempt for whom? For those poor distracted policemen? Or for their masters by whose orders they — "

"For all of them, Stani. Contempt for that besotted greed by which Joseph was once more sold by his brethren. Sold, Stani, by the very nation that should least of all have stooped to such a deed. Much may be forgiven to men whose heritage is barren rock and evil-smelling swamp, when their foul deeds betray their origin. But — Frenchmen! God's favor so bestowed imposes obligations, and they cannot be evaded without shame. Oh, Stani! How abject was the fall, when a glutted, avaricious country refused to face the test, and, with trembling hand, offered her adoptive sons. . . ."

"I know, I know. But is the nation guilty? We are here concerned with a few individuals. Don't demand too much from these poor creatures."

I could not suppress a movement of impatience.

"You are too generous, Stani. Your indulgence — "

He waved my unuttered words aside, and turned his back on me, standing by the window, his long slim outline silhouetted against the glass like a figure in a shadow theater. Then he swung round:

"Do you say that because I'm sorry for our executioners? And miserable executioners they were — I wish you could have seen them!"

A faint smile quivered on his lips.

"They opened the gate — that being the way they meant to manage it; they opened the gate, and just told us to come out. We expected to see

field grays, and when we saw they were Frenchmen
. . . gendarmes, fellows we all knew so well, I did
for a moment feel a flicker of hope — and the sight
of the sky, you know, and the trees, and freedom
— and what with that glimpse of hope, we got a
bit impatient, and began to jostle each other" —
here he grinned mirthlessly — "and push our way
out, as though, as though . . ."

He drew a deep breath and exhaled it slowly
through his teeth.

"And the first fifty — "

"Oh, Stani," I gasped. "It's horrible."

"Yes," he said; "it was horrible."

His gray eyes, deep and tender, gazed for a long
time into mine. At last I blurted out:

"And Thomas Muritz — "

Silent and motionless, with a slow droop of eyelids, he assented.

ᴄᴚᴚ

"Do you know," he went on abruptly (he had
resumed his weary pacing from wall to wall), "do
you know that when I saw him there, I was glad."

He stopped before me, spread out his hands, and
nodded his rough gray head.

"I was glad — not to be alone. I suppose — " again he began pacing to and fro — "I suppose we're all pretty selfish brutes at bottom; unless — unless it is that the human mind cannot realize that death is really there, and waiting for him: and that, in some dim fashion, I was merely glad to find a companion again — no more, and not otherwise, than I should have felt in the regiment. Perhaps that was it. But he, on the other hand, seemed appalled to see me. 'Good God! Stani!' he stuttered. 'Have they — have they — ?' I daresay, in fact, that he realized (in the exact sense of the word) the position better than I did. Perhaps because he was older. It's hard for a man still full of vigor — well, isn't it? — to shake off all his illusions.

"And yet," he went on, and then hesitated. "If he hadn't had some sort of illusions himself — how was it that he — well, I don't like to say that he broke down, but — "

He half turned and eyed me, as though he expected me to say something, or was searching my face for some sign or indication. But I did not stir.

"And yet, he had set us such an example through all those dark hours," said he, and once more he went and leaned against the window. "Such seren-

ity, such detachment. The others who were there
— alas, they did not present at all a noble spectacle. Some moaned; others — but Muritz shut
them up: a word against France, and you know
what he was like. In the end, we were all gathered
round him. And when the gate opened, when, instead of Fritzes, we saw Frenchmen — "

He fell silent, and said nothing for some seconds. He stood and stared at the great wall in front
of him, with a sort of concentrated intensity, as
though he were trying to decipher some antique
inscription blurred by time.

"Those shouts, that flash of hope, that dash for
the gateway. When Muritz got out — he was one
of the last — he looked round for me, and smiled
triumphantly.

"What did he mean?" murmured Stani in a
strange voice, as though he were demanding an
answer. "Why, the mere sight of those wretched
gendarmes' faces was enough. There was one of
them — " he thrust his hands deep into his pockets and resumed his march — "an odd little red-
haired chap with a pallid, carroty sort of complex-
ion — "

"Red-haired?"

"Well, what of it?"

"One of Muritz's emissaries. But you wouldn't understand. I'll explain later. Go on."

"Well, the expression on that man's face was plain enough. I assure you I understood pretty quick. However, Muritz went up to him with a genial smile — that genial smile of his that we all knew — and gave him two friendly taps on the shoulder; and you should have seen him jump!"

"Who? The red-haired fellow?"

"Yes: he fairly leapt into the air. And a second afterwards, he had jabbed his revolver into Muritz's ribs. Poor brute. He was scared out of his wits. 'Get up to the wall!' he yelled."

"And then — ?"

Stani stopped pacing up and down. He looked at me, but as people do look sometimes, seeing nothing. And he passed a finger slowly across his forehead.

"What followed wasn't quite so fine. It seems that Muritz — well, he suddenly collapsed. I shall never forget that scene, it was so pitiable. He stared wide-eyed at the red-haired gendarme, mumbling: 'No, no . . .' and stretching out his hands. What did he expect the man to do, in God's name? I have never seen such a look in a man's eyes. Suddenly he began to batter his fists against his temples, and wept and sobbed. God — how I wish I hadn't seen it. They shut the gate. I could still hear Muritz's voice crying 'No!' And then — "

He shuddered.

"The rattle of the Hotchkiss guns."

❧

What was I to say? Hoarse with grief and horror, I tried to get Stani to understand that those last lamentations were not, alas, those of the ultimate terror. They were — and still I sicken at the thought — the utterance of misery, despair, and horror, the agony of murdered love.

O God — why didst Thou not keep Thomas blind until the end? Why didst Thou, in that last brief moment, let him look upon that dreadful face — that face that we all bear within us, nations no less than men — the face of a being lost and forever enslaved to Mammon? Why had he to suffer? And why have I to suffer too? Since his death, not a day passes but I am tormented by the reality of his existence — and of his existence in that mortal second which not I nor anyone, none who remained worthy of his love, could spare him.

If I must henceforward bear within me the vi-

sion of what, indeed, I did not see, but nonetheless hideously insistent — the vision of that last
look, why must it overshadow my love for my own
country? Too well I know that something has gone
forever from the glory of that love. Never again,
perhaps, shall I be able to think of France with
the pure joy of days gone by. Not, indeed, by any
fault of France: but because of that last look in
the eyes of Thomas Muritz.

I also know that this will seem a matter of little
moment in the eyes of my more eminent fellow
citizens, able men who keep both their feet upon
the earth and measure a nation's greatness by its
wealth. They may even seize upon my avowal to
proclaim triumphantly that their love of France is
not to be so easily shaken. And they will give me
lessons in patriotism. What shall I reply? They will
prevail; I shall find no answer.

Night and Fog

A TRANSLATION BY HAAKON M. CHEVALIER

OF *La Nuit et le Brouillard*

BY VERCORS

I. EURYDICE

I WONDER NOW if I could not have guessed the essence of it that first day. I suppose not. Once you are initiated you are amazed that you could have been blind to so many signs. For instance, when Pierre had his hair cut. As I think about it today it seems obvious to me. But we are all good prophets, after the event.

I had barely even noticed that Pierre's hair was long. That hair, by the way . . .

The day had been a trying one. First the shock of finding his name (when I had given up all hope) on those typewritten lists, posted out in the open, which had stood off so many hopes, so many patient denials . . . Pierre Cange, of Lézardrieux. Then the shock of not being able to recognize him

— his color, as of ashes mixed with sawdust; his unbelievable emaciation; his face reduced, it seemed at first glance, to a pair of translucent ears and a nose with the skin drawn tight across the bone above the lipless mouth, his eyes round and staring, transparent and vague in their sunken hollows. His hair, on top of this — lighter, more colorless than ever — because it was long, but so sparse that the scalp showed through, like the webbing on a worn rug, made it even more evident how close this face must be to the borderline of life and death. He smiled when he saw me. Even his smile I did not recognize. Where were those dazzling teeth? He got up from his armchair, and as his tall, stiff, lanky frame draped in striped pajamas oddly unfolded he looked like a fantastic character in one of those morbid German films of the early days — a creature which some fabulous doctor has put together with pieces of corpses.

I don't remember what I said to him, but I must have been unable to conceal my feeling of shock. He smiled, but his smile did not extend to his eyes. These remained round, vague and transparent, without luster, barely expressive, barely expressing some undefined emotion — anguish perhaps, or the ghost of an old anguish.

He had just arrived. We made plans — or rather, *I* made plans. This too was unlike him, this ir- resolution, this surrender of his will into my hands. Not that he seemed to have suffered any impairment of intelligence. He answered my ques- tions with his usual sharp awareness of nuances. But where were the spontaneity, the noble energy, and the spirit of decision which we used to marvel at? Making up his mind to exercise his will seemed to have become an effort beyond his strength.

Knowing so well everything that could be call- ing him back, I imagined that he would want to return to Plenmach as soon as possible. Fully ex- pecting to see his face light up, I said:

"I'll find short cuts. We won't wait for that old Breton deportee train. When do you want to leave?"

But I could detect in his eyes, in all his features, nothing but a somewhat heightened anguish. "When?" he said in a low, hesitant voice. Then, focusing his eyes on me, he proceeded, stammering painfully, to ask a series of uncompleted questions: "What is your opinion . . . When do you think . . . Is it necessary to . . ." He lapsed into silence for a few seconds, seemed to take hold of himself, and finally said, "You think I have to go there?"

"I don't know," I said with astonishment. "You don't *have* to do *anything*. I just thought . . ." His eyes were blinking, and all at once he looked dreadfully tired. I no longer knew what to say. It's affected his will power, I decided. Suddenly it occurred to me that he had asked about all kinds of people — but not about her. This fact now struck me. *I* knew that she was all right, but did he? She, too, might have disappeared, along with so many others.

My eyes sought his, and I thought I read in them a rather heart-rending appeal. He doesn't dare to, I suddenly thought. He's afraid — what an idiot I am! — perhaps he's afraid of finding out. . . .

"Nicole is fine," I said. "She has been wonderful, up to the last day. She hasn't changed. You will find her just as she was the last time you saw her."

Yet I kept thinking as I spoke, Perhaps I'm entirely on the wrong track. Does he still love her? He never said he loved her. I was also thinking, She certainly still loves *him* — more than ever. I remembered the pathetic way she acted after Pierre was arrested. She tried valiantly to avoid giving any inkling of her despair, but a kind of poignant distraction had come over her against which her will was powerless. She tried to belie it by her animated expression, her lively movements, a determined bearing. But her days formed an unbroken chain of slips, errors, confusions, and distractions which would have been funny if they had not been so pathetic. She had taken hold of herself by degrees, and by degrees built up a strange serenity, ethereal in quality, rather similar to faith. When the sinister news from the Camp of Hochswörth had robbed us of virtually all hope, she showed more composure than any of us. She had always refused to believe that Pierre was dead.

"She will be happy to see you," I went on, "she always believed in your lucky star." I was watching Pierre curiously. But I saw nothing — or rather . . . Yes, there is a certain absence of expression which is no less surprising than some wholly unexpected expression. He kept on looking at me without saying a word, and if he did respond to my words by a vague smile, it was for all the world like a smile of politeness — and a mark of courtesy was certainly the last thing I should have expected from him under the circumstances. Could this be the only echo which the memory of Nicole awakened in him? I began to feel some concern for her.

"Naturally," I said, "it's entirely up to you. If

you prefer to stay in Paris for a while . . . Although, for your health's sake . . ."

He frowned, and his eyes moved in their sockets like those of a frightened animal. He looked at his nails (I was shocked as I noticed, for the first time, the queer shape of his fingers), then, as someone was coming in, he looked at the door; then at me once more.

Finally he spoke, lapsing into silence after every few words — every word exuding his indecision:

"In Paris? . . . I don't know . . . I'll do whatever you decide," he said, as though he were confessing to an encroaching weariness. "I leave it to you." These words seemed to have relieved him.

"Very well . . . suppose you rest up for a week," I said, hiding my astonishment. "Here, or with me. You know my house is yours. After that, depending on how strong you feel, we'll decide what to do."

"Here," he said quickly, and again his eyes were possessed by anxiety. I was completely baffled.

"Perhaps you're right," I said, to put him at ease. "They'll feed you better here. You'll get back your strength in no time."

He smiled, and gave me a look of gratitude. I realized that he had not been taken in. Well, I said to myself, seizing upon a comforting thought, at least he hasn't lost his sensitive feelers.

We arranged to meet the following day, when I would bring him some clothes. Then I took leave of him. If he had any feeling of relief at being left alone he gave no sign of it. But although I may not be particularly intuitive, I am at least sufficiently so to sense a thing of that kind.

∽

He resembled a sea gull, I decided. I wondered why I hadn't noticed it before. While he was inspecting one of his old tweed suits and his voluminous dressing robe that looks like a horse blanket, holding them up and feeling them with a childish joy that wrung my heart, I kept observing him with surprise, so unaccustomed to this new face that it seemed to me to have changed since the previous day.

He *has* changed, I said to myself suddenly. His hair . . . Yesterday it was long. He must have had it cut that very morning — very short, almost to the scalp, so that he had more the appearance of the other men moving about like uncertain shadows in the vast rooms of the building. It was short, sparse and colorless, and made him look for all the world like a sea bird.

He excused himself for a few minutes and came down again, dressed as he used to be. The familiar clothes accentuated his extreme emaciation. It was hard to believe that he had ever had that firm jaw of his, that sturdy neck. It was hard to believe that he was just over thirty. He came down the stairs holding onto the banister. His feet seemed enormous at the end of his trousers, which formed unexpected folds around his bony legs, making his whole manner of walking seem unsure, gliding, irregular, almost fear-stricken. His arms, in their voluminous sleeves, executed awkward movements as if they had constantly to re-establish the precarious equilibrium of that wretched body. . . .

We went to have a drink in the little café just opposite, on the other side of the Rue de Sèvres. It was almost a pilgrimage. A victory too, and a revenge.

"I certainly thought they had shipped you off too," said Pierre. Why of course, I said to myself (and this obvious reflection struck me as strange), of course he had no way of knowing.

It seemed funny to be telling him the story — on this very spot. Strange and yet natural. Time had simply looped the loop in space and brought us together before the little round table and the two beers which we were to have drunk at our tragically intercepted meeting two years before. On that day the object which was our signal was missing from the window of the camera shop on the corner of the boulevard. This had forewarned me. I had gone and sat on the lookout in the little *tabac* across the street. I did not really think there was any great danger: this was not our first alarm. Nevertheless I was watching for Pierre, our leader, so as to warn him. I did not have a chance to do anything. They must have arrested him right inside the station as he got off the *métro*. I barely got a glimpse of him as they brutally pushed him the short distance between the last steps and the black van (so it was waiting for *him*). I saw the raid that was being conducted at the same time in the *bistro* where I was to have met him. Some instinct made me get up; I ambled nonchalantly down to the adjoining barbershop and went in to get a shave. It was lucky for me that I did, for I learned later that the raid had taken in all the cafés in the neighborhood and all the men on the sidewalks.

Pierre was gazing at the subway entrance, listen-

ing to the hoarse cries of the women selling newspapers. One of them (was it intentional?) kept
repeating, *"Libération! Ce Soir, le Monde et
Libres!"* [1] He smiled as he contemplated this scene
of peacetime animation — without Germans, without menace.

"It's hard to believe," he said. I don't know
whether he was speaking of that moment or of the
other, from which these two years separated us.
He looked at his left hand, the sight of which had
been such a shock to me. He spoke again: "Whom
did they arrest after me?"

"No one," I smiled. "You know that."

He looked at me. I cannot describe his expression. It contained gratitude, pride, and deep joy
as well as distress and heartbreak, but to tell the
truth I was quite unable to recognize this at the
time, though I was deeply troubled by it.

"No one?" he said, and again he looked at his
mutilated hand and added, "How was I to know?"
But the words came timidly, with the disarming
guile which an unassuming person may resort to
when he wishes to be complimented.

[1] The names of underground newspapers. Because the
pronunciation of *est* (is) and *et* (and) is similar, the news
vendor seems to be shouting, "Liberation! Tonight the
world is free!"

I laid it on thick. "Are you under the impression that we were completely in the dark? Everything that goes on in prison leaks out, and we always found out everything — the coincidences and lucky encounters, the failures, the heroism. You ask how you could have known that all of us escaped. Our safety depended on your not revealing our names to your torturers. At the end of the second day you jumped through the window. If it hadn't been for that providential balcony, you would not be here. If it hadn't been for your courage, I would not be here either. So you see, we know everything."

Pierre was looking straight ahead. On the strip of ground along the sidewalk a child was pushing a toy wheelbarrow.

"I jumped because I was afraid I'd give in," Pierre murmured. He was watching the child, who was pretending to empty his wheelbarrow and then to refill it. "They had already more than half done me in. Then they left me in a cell for six hours — to imagine what was to follow. When they came to fetch me I was afraid I might weaken." He turned his head and, for the first time, riveted his eyes on me with that look I knew so well.

"But I wasn't thinking of you at all," he went on.

He fastened his eyes on me with an intense scrutiny. "I was only thinking of them, my torturers — *of them and of myself*. What they were going to do to me." He looked away. The corner of his pallid lips trembled ever so slightly. His eyes seemed to recede even more, to harden and darken.

"They weren't just out to make us talk. They were not merely policemen. They were playing another game, too. A premeditated, cruel, and relentless game. The forfeit was our souls."

A large car drew up to the curb in front of us. From it emerged a man in uniform, plump and nonchalant, with four braids on his sleeve. He went off to buy a newspaper. In the car a woman with blond hair hanging loosely to her shoulders, Hollywood fashion, was waiting for him. She affected an air of superiority and boredom.

"Life or death is a small matter," Pierre continued. "Ours, I mean, and also yours, which were partly in our hands. They saw it pretty clearly. From that day on I understood what they were after."

His gaze fell on me for a moment. "Did you have any idea of their fiendish purpose?"

"Are you referring," I ventured, "to extermination . . .?"

"Oh, extermination. . . ." It was an interruption, but on a mild and relaxed note. He brushed the word aside with a movement of his bony hand. "A dead man is a dead man. Furthermore, alive or dead, men like ourselves still count for something — for something which death does not cancel. They knew that, all right," he said softly, as if lost in reverie; then, louder, with a dry, bitter hardness, "They knew that, all right, they knew that perfectly well. What they wanted was to turn us into rags. And when you're a rag there's just nothing left of you," he said, emphasizing each word. And he lifted toward the sky a nose so frail, with the skin so transparent, that one could clearly see where the bone ended and the cartilage began. His lids contracted slightly in the light. "I'm not speaking of the body. If your body is reduced to a rag, you die or you recover." He smiled. "Take me, for instance — what they didn't break themselves was smashed by my fall. Aside from this hand, which is a complete mess, the rest has patched itself together and is back to normal, or just about."

He paused, with his mouth half-open, then went on, "As for giving away a name, an address . . . Ah, I wonder if that really meant so much to them — I wonder if it meant very much even to us. Don't misunderstand," he explained quietly. "You realize of course that . . . But," he continued without transition, and he thrust forward his thin nose and his round eyes — he really did look like a sea gull — "whether we gave it away or not was the crucial thing. That was the whole battle. The one who held out, no matter how badly crippled, remained wholly himself. But the one who flinched . . ." His face, as he turned to me, was lighted by a kind of grave smile. "I didn't give anything away," he said simply. "But I wonder what life must be like for one who has betrayed his comrades. He's nothing but a rag. A creature who has become degraded in his own eyes is nothing but a rag. Death is a hundred times better."

I thought of our many comrades whose nerves had failed them (and of myself too, of the question which I had so often asked myself, of my inability to answer it), and I suggested, "Aren't you being too severe? One failure doesn't necessarily prove . . ."

"Oh," he broke in, with such vehemence that for the first time I recognized, I saw flare up again, that lofty disdain, that haughty arrogance — yes, that pride — which for two days I had been vainly hoping to discover, "I'm speaking of men like myself."

∾

I received no letter from him, but I did not expect any. I had put him on the train the fifteenth of June. A short note from Jean-Jacques had reassured me as to his safe arrival. Everything was fine, he said. At Plenmach they had found Pierre less shattered than they had feared. Every day he was improving, physically. I balked a little at this word: was the qualification intentional? The postscript certainly seemed to indicate as much. "Nicole is happy," her brother wrote — "as happy as she can be, at least. Pierre's behavior is rather strange."

I can't say that I was altogether surprised by this, but it saddened me. I had counted a good deal on what getting back would do for him. I was disappointed and worried.

All this more or less slipped out of my mind while I impatiently wound up the things that were still keeping me in Paris. I finally left for Brittany, to settle down on the little island near Bréhat which I had not seen for five years. It is not far from Plenmach and I was glad of this. But when I got there I found that it would be several days before I could get away. There were too many things that needed to be put back into shape, including, first of all, means of transportation: my little cutter which badly needed calking, and a rather damaged punt.

After so long an absence, need I mention the endless hours I spent out on the rocks during those first days? I never tired of looking at the sea, nor at the archipelago, at that landscape filled with magic which the tide was continually transforming. It was nine o'clock one evening and still broad daylight, but the setting sun cast upon the calm waters the blue transparent shadows of the rocks. I drank in the silence and the soft light. I was watching the waters of the Trieux slowly descending toward me with the tide. A small skiff was descending with them, getting little or no help from the feeble breeze. I watched it as it drifted, distant and calm, with the feeling of friendliness and warmth which the merest rowboat awakens in me. The light was behind it and at first I did not notice the color of the sail. Then I discovered that it was flame-colored, and when I observed that the

jib was blue I frowned. Those had been the colors
of Jean-Jacques's little sloop, and I often recognized it from afar by its colors. But how could it
be he this evening? Not that I was surprised at
Jean-Jacques's coming to see me. He always used
to enjoy such visits. But not like this, at the end
of the day, when the sea had barely begun to ebb.
The tide would not be rising toward Lézardrieux
again for a good six hours. How could he hope to
get back to Plenmach before nightfall with so little
wind — against weather and tide?

He it was, nevertheless. There could no longer
be any doubt. The small craft was approaching in
the twilight glimmer, and its slow, soundless movement evoked that sense of peace and simple joy
which comes to me each time as a fresh experience.
Tonight, however, it was mixed with a feeling of
uneasiness. This visit was quite out of the ordinary.

Taking advantage of a small gust of wind, the
man in the boat braced his sail and, cutting across
the current, headed directly for the little pier on
the south shore of the island. I went down to help
moor the boat. It *was* Jean-Jacques. He waved a
greeting. As the boat slowly drifted in he began
to lower the sails.

"Leave some slack for the tide," he said, throwing me the hawser, and while I was making it fast to a ringbolt, he began to lash the mainsail to the boom. All this certainly proved that he planned to spend the night on the island.

It was so unusual that I did not know how to greet him. I put on a big smile of welcome, but at the same time did not try to hide my astonishment and curiosity. He looked at my face with a kind of avid interest, then jumped onto the pier and pulled off his boots. He got up, looked at me again, and asked:

"Isn't he here?"

The anxiety in his voice was in itself an answer.

"Who?" I asked, and for a moment I was really racking my brain.

He took me by the arm and suggested, "Let's go inside," and we walked up toward the house. We had not taken ten steps, of course, before I knew, in spite of Jean-Jacques's silence, that he was speaking of Pierre.

I set out a little table on the close-clipped grass, and two of those handy Moroccan armchairs. There was a thrill in the deepening twilight. The sky was clear, the softly stirring wind almost warm. I had discovered a bottle of Calvados, and

I had some cigars which a friend had brought me from Switzerland.

"To tell you the truth, I didn't have too much hope of finding him here," said Jean-Jacques. "But it was a hope, just the same. I wonder where he can be."

"When did he disappear?"

"We found his room empty this morning."

He really looked worried.

"You can't have expected to keep him cooped up!" I remarked.

"At any other time," he began, making a gesture that signified "Of course not!" He shook his head. Then he said, "It's strange, his going off like this, I'm telling you."

"Was there nothing that could have made you anticipate it?" I asked.

"Nothing," he repeated, and there was concern in his voice. "Well, perhaps . . . and yet I didn't anticipate it." After a moment's silence he said, "His mother is beside herself."

"What about Nicole?" I ventured.

"Oh, you know how she is. She won't give in to anxiety. At least — " he smiled — "to look at her. . . . She says just what you say — that after all he isn't our prisoner."

"Does she still love him?" I asked bluntly.

"Yes."

"And he?" I slowly tapped the ashes from my cigar.

His eyes followed the little taps attentively, as though his answer depended on them, and he said:

"I'd swear to it."

"Well?"

He did not answer. He seemed to be completely absorbed in sipping his drink. By now the night had closed in on us and we were speaking like two shadows. The silence lengthened. He was diligently smoking his cigar.

"You saw him in Paris, didn't you?" he finally asked, the words coming slowly. I nodded. "Didn't you find him — odd?"

"In a way," I admitted. "But . . ."

Jean-Jacques rose to his feet and, going down close to the edge, tossed the butt of his cigar into the water with a great sweep of his arm. It sizzled faintly as it went out.

"In a way," he said, echoing my words and looking at me. He was still standing, and now began to pace back and forth with short steps, head bowed, kicking up small clods with the toes of his shoes.

"In a way. You're very cautious with your words. Yes, he is odd, in a way. For instance, when . . . Damn it, I call that being out of one's mind!" he exploded. He stopped, squarely facing me, his legs apart. "I expected a lot of changes, especially physical ones. Well, it's just . . . You did the right thing, I think; he looked fine when he arrived. You did the right thing in keeping him there for over a month."

"You don't think *I* had anything to do with it!" I protested.

"With postponing his return? Wasn't that your idea?"

"I was the one who pushed him into the train. He would still be there if I had waited for him to make up his mind."

The shadow in front of me, outlined against the sea and the sky where the last gleams of light were dying before the utter darkness, remained for a long moment motionless and silent.

"Yes, I should have suspected it . . ." He was talking to himself rather than to me. "Why of course!" he said as if a sudden light had dawned on him, and again he began to pace slowly up and down.

"And then his not writing. Only one letter. Do

you know that he wrote Nicole *one* letter, just one? And when I say 'letter' . . . She couldn't help showing it to me. Poor little thing, what she must have gone through to bring herself to . . . you know how proud she is, how reserved . . . but the ordeal of that letter was more than she could face alone. What a riddle!

> NICOLE,
> A ghost has returned to the world of men, a ghost which no longer even has the strength to drink from the pure springs of memory. Ah, give him time, and until then do not write, do not come. And forgive your
>
> PIERRE

I know every word of it by heart," he said as though he had just discovered the fact, and he fell silent.

He was probably waiting for me to answer the unspoken question put to me by his motionless silence.

"It's certainly strange," I finally admitted.

I heard a kind of repressed laugh.

"I'll say it is. It doesn't make sense. Is he breaking with her? No. The contrary? Not that either. Why did he write? And, having written, why the devil did he come? If he no longer loved her . . .

but he does love her. Well, then, if he loves her
. . . why doesn't he say so!"

"And yet," I ventured, "when he left I thought
he seemed less . . . harassed, more well-bal-
anced . . ."

"Exactly!" Jean-Jacques exclaimed with utter
stupefaction. "That's exactly it."

That was what he could not understand, he explained. When he went to meet him at the train he
was expecting to see a Pierre who would be taciturn, or in low spirits, or else impatient, irritable.
. . . But nothing of the sort. The man who got
off the train at Paimpol seemed almost jovial, and
in any case alert and calm. They embraced. As
there was no gasoline to be had, the old St. Gouëno
carriage had been brought out and harnessed. It
takes at least an hour in this conveyance to travel
from Paimpol to Lézardrieux, and a good fifteen
minutes more to reach Plenmach. Pierre wanted
to drive.

"Haven't had my hand on a wheel in five years,
and I haven't had the feel of a pair of reins in
twenty!" He drove fast, through the fog and the
drizzle — real Breton weather. On the downgrades,
instead of using the brakes he urged the old nag
on at full speed, and the carriage bounced right

and left on its high wheels and worn springs, with a din of metal and creaking wood. Pierre was delighted: his eyes, his reflexes, were as alert as ever. "Not so far gone as all that, am I?" From time to time, when the overtaxed old horse showed signs of fatigue, he would draw the antique cariole up to the side of the road, jump out and gaze over the heath, or at least as much of it as could be seen looming, gray and blurred, through the mist. Pierre breathed the air deeply and smiled. "Everything that I love . . ."

Jean-Jacques would have liked to talk about that famous letter, but he did not dare. He declared, by way of leading up to it, that he was pleasantly surprised at the way Pierre looked, for he had been worried.

Pierre smiled. "Yes," he said, "I'm beginning to get back. The physical and the mental go together, as everyone knows. It's a matter of time. In Paris I spent some very dark days, and nursed some even darker thoughts. Thank God, I have shaken them off and I left them there, along with my discarded clothes."

Jean-Jacques felt that the moment had come. "Nicole," he ventured, "has been in such a state all morning . . ." He looked at Pierre, scrutinizing the face half obliterated by the shadow of the black carriage top. Pierre at first said nothing. Even his smile did not vanish immediately. He kept on driving, through the fog, at a pace which Jean-Jacques himself found a bit reckless. He kept on talking, too, but it seemed as if his very spirit were sinking into the night, and his answers came in ambiguous and vague and lagging phrases, ever more lagging — like a cart which one pushes along a muddy road and which bogs down deeper and deeper until finally it gets hopelessly stuck. Presently Jean-Jacques no longer had the strength to keep it going, and silence filled the somber, jolting carriage, with the fading daylight clinging to the dusty panes. The horse, no longer urged, settled down to a lazy jog, and the sound of the hoofs came at ever greater intervals, like the tick of a metronome running down. The carriage rolled along in this way for some time, of its own momentum — and then stopped. There was a black silence. Finally Pierre turned his head and gave his friend a queer look, blinking slightly as he did so.

"Listen . . ." he said and his indistinct face broke into a hesitant smile, like an apology, and also like a pathetic appeal for understanding and help. Two or three times he parted his lips, drawing in his breath, as a person does when he cannot make up his mind to speak. Finally he managed to say:

"Listen . . . not tonight. Is that impossible? Not tonight. Tomorrow."

Jean-Jacques understood perfectly. It's beginning all over again, he thought, and he exclaimed:

"But she's expecting you, old man."

Pierre turned his head away and looked at his hands, which he held in his lap. "I am tired," he said pitifully, "I should have liked . . . I'm only asking for a little time."

Jean-Jacques could no longer contain himself. "Listen, old man . . ."

But Pierre, with a crack of the reins, brusquely threw the horse into a gallop, so obviously determined to interrupt what would follow that Jean-Jacques left the words unspoken.

They rode on thus in silence, but now Pierre drove at an unhurried pace in the gathering twilight. It was as though he wished to let the night overtake him and become dense enough to cloak his arrival. And when the carriage started down the long avenue lined with horse chestnuts, the trees actually did appear a little hallucinatory and unreal in the flickering light of the lanterns.

At a turn in the road Jean-Jacques caught sight of a furtive white figure among the trees. "Nicole," he said to himself, and he turned to look back through the small rear window. He saw her running, looking a little ghostlike in the fog. He put his hand on Pierre's arm to have him stop the carriage and leaned out of the door. He saw nothing. But suddenly he felt his companion give a start, with a brusque movement that threw him back even further into the shadow. He turned round. Framed in the other window was the face of Nicole, peering through the dusty glass, with an agonizing expression of mingled hope and terror. Yet he hardly had time to let it register ("For the rest of my life, probably," he whispered) before Pierre Cange feverishly snapped the reins. Almost immediately, as if she herself had been struck by the reins, Nicole faded into the shadowy mist, disappearing so suddenly that her brother, the next moment, wondered in all sincerity if it had not been merely an illusion.

"And perhaps that is what I would have believed," he informed me, "if I had not caught a fleeting glimpse of the slender white figure vanishing among the trees as the old horse, left to himself, started off at a sleepy pace. Inside the slow-moving, jogging carriage the silence grew so dense and so heavy that I imagined I could hear it. . . . But what I heard was the sound of Pierre's breathing. All I could see of him in the dim light of the lanterns, as he sat huddled far back under the carriage top, was the pale glow of his hands on his knees, clutching the reins. He was breathing. Each breath seemed to be an effort. He was breathing. Without letup. In the darkness of the broken-down, creaking, and jolting rattletrap, surrounded by mist, night, and rain, the sound was almost more than I could bear."

∾

In the night — now black as ink, with only his white sweater still dimly visible, headless and armless, like some Greek torso submerged in water — Jean-Jacques spoke in a voice all muffled with reverie. And in this mute, balmy, infinitely motionless darkness, the strange images suggested by his words took on for me who was listening as from the depth of a specious sleep the persuasive power of a dream.

Pierre's mother, smiling but looking a little

worn, was waiting on the front steps. Behind her,
Nicole was now standing motionless in the half-
open doorway, a blurred, wan shape in the darkness of the porch. Pierre drew up the carriage and
got out. He took a few steps and stopped at the
bottom of the stairs. Madame Cange did not at
once recognize the tall, thin form. Then she said,
"Mon Dieu," and burst into tears. She came down,
putting both feet on each step, and threw herself
sobbing on his narrow chest. Pierre pressed her to
him, telling her all sorts of nice things, but he did
not kiss her.

"No, he didn't," said Jean-Jacques, and this was
still another example of his strange behavior to
which he said he could find no clue. Pierre held
his mother tight, murmuring warm and tender
words, but he did not kiss her — and his eyes remained fastened on Nicole. He was looking at her
as if to say, "You see, I am not kissing her." And
Nicole, with those eyes upon her, first turned all
pink and then all pale. And when Pierre finally let
go of his mother the girl did not move. She remained there in the doorway, silent and motionless, her eyes dilated. Pierre climbed the steps,
with his mother on his arm. He only climbed the
steps and there he stopped and said softly, "Hello,

101

Nicole." And she answered, "Hello, Pierre" — but without moving, just like that. Pierre seemed to be waiting. Then Nicole drew back from the door and Pierre went inside, without touching her, without even holding out his hand to her. He smiled, and Nicole smiled too, and it was not exactly a sad smile, but a rather pathetic smile just the same, the courageous but almost tearful smile of lovers looking at each other through the window of a train.

A supper had been set out in the large living room. But Pierre asked to be allowed to go to bed without waiting, on the ground that he was exhausted from his journey. "What, not even a moment?" Madame Cange protested. "Not even ten minutes?"

"Tomorrow, Mother, please," said Pierre, "I am really very weary." The words were addressed to his mother, but he was looking at Nicole. "I am not yet . . . as . . . strong . . ." He made a movement and glanced at Jean-Jacques. "I misjudged my strength, I'm afraid . . ." he said slowly, with a melancholy smile, and added, "It'll be better tomorrow. Every day I'll be better. It just takes time, only a little time," he repeated, as he had done in the carriage. He went to the foot of the stairs, of the oak staircase which rose in a spiral to the inner balcony. "Forgive me," he said, addressing the company once more, and grasping the banister he climbed the first steps, then gradually disappeared in the dark. Nicole had half lifted one arm, without smiling. Madame Cange stared, red-eyed, into the shadowy recesses of the room where the sound of the footsteps was dying away. Jean-Jacques said he would go out and fetch the baggage, and it was with relief that he left the silent room.

⌀⌀

Such was their first meeting — "and it may perhaps explain," Jean-Jacques mused aloud, "why Pierre and Nicole were so pitifully unable to draw close to each other after that. And yet they love each other," he repeated with utter conviction. "Good God, haven't I seen . . ." he began, only to fall back once again into one of his silent reveries. He came out of it only to repeat that he "just couldn't understand it." He was not even able to put two and two together and make them add up to four. Nicole's attitude he somehow managed to account for — she was a proud, high-strung

girl, gifted with the kind of intuition which is beyond the comprehension of us poor males with
our logic and all the things that bog us down. "Perhaps she has figured it all out, but she won't say
a word." As for him, no matter how hard he tried
he still couldn't figure it out, he just couldn't.

Pierre kept to his room. What did he do there?
He wasn't writing, and certainly the library of
Plenmach could not help him fill those solitary
hours. It was exactly like a prolonged sulking spell.
Yet he came down very regularly for meals, where
he showed a smiling countenance and a manner
which was affectionately attentive toward his
mother, friendly toward Jean-Jacques, perfectly
polite and respectful toward Nicole. No, there
was nothing that one could object to, unless . . .
"It was a perfectly acceptable attitude, except
coming from him," said Jean-Jacques as though
this were an explanation. And to anyone who had
known Pierre — his warmth, the appealing frank-
ness, the open cordiality, the absence of solemnity
which he showed in his relations with people —
it *was* an explanation. It was only after dinner that
he spent a little time in the company of the other
members of the household. Every evening some
neighbor would drop in to congratulate him on his

return. Pierre would remain, but his presence, which had once been so stimulating, at times so inspiring, was now but the source of an oppressive perplexity. He would sit in one of the large tapestry-covered armchairs near the oak staircase, and Jean-Jacques noticed that he always was careful to keep his face somewhat in the shadow. He would cross his long thin legs and then remain motionless, impassive and motionless.

Nicole, too, generally remained silent, her head bowed over the frayed fish net which she was mending (in the hope, as her brother might plausibly assume, of reviving Pierre's interest in sea fishing). But she would look up with something akin to embarrassment when anyone spoke to her and fasten upon him her dark slate-colored eyes whose dreamy light seemed to shimmer and waver like moonlight. At other times, letting the great triple-meshed net drop to her knees, so that her hands seemed to be caught in its folds, and lifting her narrow forehead framed by the luxuriant copper hair which took on a vapory sheen in the lamplight, she would fix her gaze, now neither wavering nor shimmering, but intense and motionless, on the dark corner where Pierre's face was hidden.

This was how those strange evenings were spent.

On one occasion Jean-Jacques had climbed to the inner balcony to lower the chandelier for Madame Cange, who wanted more light for her sewing. It was a large Dutch chandelier, that could be raised or lowered by means of a pulley, the cord of which attached to one of the balusters. Being thus himself in the shadow, Jean-Jacques noticed that he could make out Pierre's face more clearly. "Pierre's face . . ." he repeated, and he gave a faint laugh, tinged with melancholy. "Yes, a face of stone. A real stone face, imperturbable and cold. But those eyes!" They glowed in the dark, he told me, with the fixity of a cat's. They were looking at Nicole. It was so startling that Jean-Jacques, instead of going down again, remained motionless in the darkness, his eyes fascinated by those eyes which were riveted on Nicole. He sensed that Pierre's obstinate stare did not just originate at this moment, but that every evening, exactly as this evening, every evening since the first evening Pierre from his point of vantage in the shadow must have been peering at the girl in this way. The thought of it overwhelmed him and he was still standing there, in a turmoil of emotions, when Madame Cange put aside her work and got up, taking with her that day's visitor, who was interested in architecture and who had expressed a wish to see the vaulted cellars of Plenmach. For the first time the two young people were left alone — or so they thought.

Then Nicole, letting the net enmesh her hands on her knees as she often did, once again raised her eyes to that face hidden in the dark. She could not see it, but perhaps — without any doubt — she guessed that by this penetrating gaze she was responding to that invisible gaze. She was pale, she seemed to hesitate, yet one could barely perceive a faint quiver of her eyelids. Finally she said:

"Pierre . . ."

Jean-Jacques saw the lids brusquely lower over the eyes gleaming in the dark. As though they might afford him a shelter against his own weakness. But he did not answer, did not budge. Nicole hesitated. Jean-Jacques could see her fingers trembling under the net.

"Pierre . . . you're not asleep?"

The answer took time in coming, but it finally came, in a whisper tinged with bitterness.

"I'm not asleep, no. I'm not asleep."

Then Nicole, in a soft voice expressing at once her passion and her grief, answered tremblingly,

"You are suffering, Pierre, and I can't help you."

"No, you can't. Not now," was all he said.

"You have not even shaken my hand, not even touched me with a finger," said Nicole strangely. "Not once."

To Jean-Jacques's surprise Pierre sprang to his feet. He crossed the room, dragging his feet, which were too heavy for him. A fleeting light shone in Nicole's eyes. But Pierre's movements became slower, he stopped, and squatted and sat down at the girl's feet. He took a section of the great net and buried his fingers in its meshes.

"I used to put my hand in yours," said Nicole, "and when you closed it the whole of mine would fit inside."

Pierre was playing with the net, spreading his fingers fanwise, and he hardly seemed to hear her. As for Jean-Jacques, he was in the throes of a dozen conflicting emotions, torn between an overpowering curiosity and the sense of committing a shameless indiscretion. But he was unable even to move a finger, paralyzed by his indecision as much as by the fear of revealing his unwarranted presence so belatedly.

Pierre lowered his hands and extricated his fingers. He gazed at Nicole with that expression of anxiety which made him look so much like a sea bird, and asked:

"Do you still like green frogs, Nicole?"

The girl seemed no less surprised than Jean-Jacques by the incongruous question. In an uncertain voice she answered, "Yes, still . . ."

"But you couldn't bring yourself to touch one, could you? You never could. You like them, but you can't stand touching them."

"That's true," she agreed. "But, Pierre, why . . ."

"Not even with the tip of your finger, can you?"

"Oh, Pierre . . ." she murmured, "do I affect you that way — like a frog?"

He let go the net and jumped to his feet.

"Good God!" he said in great agitation, "how can you think . . ."

He had extended his good hand toward her, but he pulled it back almost immediately, and as if under a sudden compulsion hid it behind his back. And it was his other hand, the crushed hand with the shapeless fingers, which he reached out, and with infinite tenderness he stroked her fine copper hair, so lightly as barely to graze it. Nicole wanted to seize this hand, but he had already withdrawn it. He shook his head slowly three times and looked down at her. His glance was heavy with things unspoken.

"Oh, Pierre, Pierre," she whispered, "is it because of your hand? Give it to me, let me hold it against my cheek."

He hesitated, smiled, and slowly extended it to her. It was a red, deformed hand, really rather horrible. Nicole pressed it to her downturned face.

"Give me . . . the other one." To Jean-Jacques's surprise he detected apprehension, fear, in her murmured plea. And sure enough, Pierre firmly pulled back his hand, turned, and walked away. Nicole let her hands fall back into her lap, where they lay like fish caught in the net stretched across her knees. With slow steps Pierre went over to the window. The minutes seemed endless as he stood looking at the black sky. Behind him he must have felt Nicole's anxious and persistent gaze.

"Don't ask any questions — ever," he murmured.

Nicole stared for a long time at his pale, shrunken neck before she answered in a low voice, "And yet we've got to cure you."

Pierre wheeled round and shouted:

"Not you!"

The girl's eyes, enlarged but calm, had continued to rest on him. He lowered his own, as if to give himself time, then looked up again and tried to smile.

"Soon . . ." he said, with a controlled effort, "when I have gotten . . . everything will be all right." He repeated, as though he were trying to convince himself, "Everything will be . . . quite . . . quite all right." He stuck out his chin with an air of assurance — the effect was pitiful — and added, "Soon. Yes, I'm sure of it." Nicole closed her eyes with a look of pain and turned her face away.

Pierre remained leaning against the window, his tall figure outlined against the night. With surprising clearness his emaciated face expressed a determined hope, a touching energy, which the turned-down corners of his mouth somewhat belied. Nicole had gone back to her work, but her hands trembled and at times the knots became tangled between her fingers. Under the spell of this silence Jean-Jacques in his dark corner hardly dared to breathe.

And then Madame Cange returned, followed by her guest. Pierre hastened to resume his place in the shadow. And while his mother and her guest carried on their inconsequential chatter, he once more fastened on Nicole the luminous eyes of a watchful, patient cat.

"Then suddenly I couldn't stand it any longer," Jean-Jacques exclaimed, and, as if the same impatience were again getting the better of him, he got up nervously and strode off to gaze at the sea. The moon had risen behind Bréhat and the strange forms of the rocks of the archipelago were outlined in black against the shimmering silver of the incredibly calm water. It suggested some prehistoric landscape, another planet. There was not a breath of wind. The sky was but a cloud of stardust.

"I was all on edge," he said. "I could no more have kept myself from butting in than I could from spying on them a few minutes before. I shifted my position up there, to make some noise. Nicole's eyes fluttered, she raised her hands from her lap and bowed her head over her work. Pierre's face lifted a little and his eyes tried to make me out in the dark. I came down the stairs and went over to him. "Let's take a little turn outside, Pierre. It's a wonderful night." Even his mother, even the visitor (that night it was Captain Dhoué — you know, who runs the boat for the Bridges and Highways Commission) reacted to the unusual character of this proposal under the circumstances.

I tried to avoid Nicole's glance, but I could almost feel it glued to my neck — avid, trembling, and terrified. Pierre slowly uncrossed his legs, and then he got up, with a hesitant slowness. "It will do you good," I said, with a rather forced offhandedness. He remained standing for a moment, looking at me sideways, just long enough for me to see the corner of one extremely penetrating and lively eye. He opened his mouth.

"Take something to put around your neck!" Madame Cange exclaimed. Pierre smiled, and went over and took a Scotch wool scarf off a hook. I had already opened the door. We went out, and as I closed the door behind us I caught a glimpse of Nicole beneath the lamplight, like a vision in a dream, with her hands and the net drawn up to her bosom. Thus she looked as though she had been completely caught in its meshes, a nymph or a Nereid miraculously fished out of the sea, and whose dilated eyes sent out a mute appeal in which terror and hope were mingled.

ോ

The heath around Plenmach, under the cover of night, had the awe-inspiring aspect which formerly, when they used to venture over it as children, would fill their hearts with a delightful thrill, composed of panic and the unavowed desire to witness sudden apparitions or other supernatural phenomena. Today the two men walked in silence, once again in the grip, Jean-Jacques confessed — yes, in the grip of a kind of fear. Only this fear sprang from themselves and not from the heath.

The silence between them was thickening, and Jean-Jacques clearly felt that each minute lost made the effort to break it harder. He seized Pierre's wrist, and as he did so his friend turned to him a face on which dread was written. But it was already too late, the words had already sprung from his lips:

"You love her, don't you?"

Immediately the dread disappeared. As may happen, not when fear has chosen the wrong object, but when the object becomes a reality, apprehension gives way to the resolve to defend oneself. As he watched Pierre's eyes in the light of the stars and the crescent moon, Jean-Jacques saw — even though they were riveted on his — something like the iron shutter of a shop window come down over them.

"Don't try," said Pierre in a hoarse voice.

The words were uttered in such a way that they suggested many others. The announcement that the effort was wasted: "What's the use? I won't answer." A warning — a counsel and a plea: "Not this way: danger." A threat: "Look out!" An entreaty: "Spare me."

The two men were still facing each other. Jean-Jacques was a little taken aback. Pierre did not try to free himself from his grasp. His eyes had again assumed their impenetrable expression. Once more his whole face had turned to bronze. Jean-Jacques shook his arm violently, as one does to a child who refuses to understand.

"Why, you confounded . . . Damn it all! Don't you understand that I'm trying to help you?"

In answer, silence.

"Do you think I didn't see you?"

Pierre smiled. "So? Very fine. My congratulations."

"God Almighty, she loves you, she's my sister. I'm willing to bet anything you love her too. What is all this business? What are you getting at? Damn it to hell! She's a human being, a child! Don't you realize you're torturing her?"

"Yes, I'm torturing her," Pierre admitted in a low voice, but distinctly.

"Well!" Jean-Jacques was choking. "Really! . . . well, that's a good one! You know it and yet you keep right on! My God, if it's marriage you're afraid of . . ."

"You fool!" said Pierre plainly and calmly.

"Good," Jean-Jacques retorted. "I'm delighted to accept the epithet. But then why this damned silence? You know I can understand anything, but after all . . . look at the child . . . Hell and damnation, it can't go on! It's as if you were trying to . . . as if you didn't dare . . . either to win her or lose her. Well, that doesn't go any more. You've got to either win her or lose her. I'm responsible for . . . For heaven's sake, can't you say a word?"

He was still holding Pierre's wrist, holding it firmly. The latter made no effort to free himself. But he took a deep breath and said:

"I beg of you — wait a while. Just wait a while."

And suddenly, in a feverish voice:

"Don't you understand that I'm . . . oh, Jean-Jacques, my old brother. I'm like a . . . a climber clinging to the wall of a mountain, dogged but out of breath. He can still climb, but only by clenching his teeth. Don't ask me to talk . . . not now. Later, when I've . . ." He stopped, as though

116

he were really out of breath. He took two or three deep breaths before he could add, ". . . scaled the heights, from which I can at last . . . at last . . ." And suddenly he exclaimed, "I'll get there! I'll tear myself loose from this sinister valley full of fog! I'll scale those crystal heights again, I'll breathe that limpid air, I'll drink my fill of that icy brightness! Who is going to prevent me?"

"Who is preventing you?" Jean-Jacques asked. This grandiloquence had irritated him. He had not released Pierre's wrist, and now he felt it tremble.

"You're like Hamlet," he said, perhaps cruelly, "you unburden your heart with words. You no longer know how to act."

For the first time Pierre made a violent effort to release the hold on his wrist. But Jean-Jacques kept a firm grip. "You no longer dare to act!" he repeated, for he felt a kind of anger welling within him. "Nicole isn't the only subject of my speech, I want you to know! No, no, you're going to listen to me to the end," he announced as though he read a mute entreaty in Pierre's reaction. "You've been here now for weeks, refusing everything. Do you think France has a superabundance of men like you? Just today, for instance . . ."

Jean-Jacques told me that as he was about to go on he had an intuition that he would better have left his thoughts unspoken. But men blush to obey their instinct if reason does not come to their support.

"Keeping to yourself the way you do!" he continued. "Refusing to see anyone! Do you know what those four young fellows this morning wanted?"

"I already told you . . ." Pierre broke in in a nervous voice, as if he were afraid of what was coming.

". . . that you don't want to hear about it, I know. Well, whether you want to or not, you're going to hear it. It's all too stupid!" he exclaimed with angry impatience, and the words began to pour forth: "Damn it all, I'm going to get you out of this, whether you want it or not. Who were those boys? Four survivors of Buchenwald. Full of memories that you left there, before you were taken to Hochswörth. They sang your praises. They built altars to you. They were inexhaustible. You should have seen your mother, and Nicole! . . . What did they want? They've formed an association in St. Brieux which is bringing together all the Bretons of the camp. They want you to be their president. There you are. They want you to take them in hand as you did in Buchenwald. They won't be put off, I'm warning you. They told me as much. They'll bide their time."

"He tore himself loose from the grasp of my fingers," Jean-Jacques said, "as though they had been red-hot iron. There was a moment of deep immobility, and a silence . . . a silence . . . as heavy as lead. And then he whispered (I almost had to read the words on his lips), 'Not another word.' And, by Jove, I didn't find another word to say. We stood there face to face, transformed into statues of salt. At last Pierre slowly raised a hand, and first he withdrew a step or two, backwards. Then he seemed to sidle, crabwise, in the direction of the slope, with the slow veering of a ship left to the mercy of the winds. As he turned, he kept his hand extended toward me, and also his strange look. This is the last sight I had of his face. And then I saw nothing more than his back going down the heath. He moved away so quickly that he disappeared in the dark as though the night had engulfed him."

༭

I remained for a long time, in the balmy darkness of this summer night, silently turning over in my mind the somber imaginings which this story stirred up. Fatigue and the night combined led my confused thoughts close to the border of hallucination, and the wind with its heavy sea odors blended, in this melancholy reverie, with the pathetic struggle for survival which the unhappy Pierre had been waging for twenty days, while the cold moonbeams became in their turn the bitter discovery that he would never succeed. For there seemed to be no doubt that Pierre had given up the fight, and his flight this morning was the admission of his defeat.

I don't know in what kind of reverie Jean-Jacques, for his part, was engaged. I do know that he murmured, with slow deliberation, "Fool. Fool," and I heard three short mocking sighs. "Not to have had sense enough to realize that he would run away! It's true that none of the rest of them . . . except Nicole, oh! Nicole . . ."

I got up. The moon was high in the sky.

"Why did you think he might be here?"

"He took the rowboat. The one he used to use to raise his lobster pots. The people out at the Bodic lighthouse saw him this morning at dawn go down with the tide. We hoped . . . but he took too many things with him, one day's fishing doesn't require so much — he's certainly going off to hide somewhere. I'll go and look around in Bréhat tomorrow."

I hesitated before venturing:

"Do you think it's very wise to interfere?"

"Inaction is never wise."

The night hid Jean-Jacques from me, but I could imagine his melancholy smile: Pierre Cange himself was answering me. These words belonged to his legend. I felt deeply their irony and their bitterness.

11. ORPHEUS

HE DRANK the potion and was seized with a fit of coughing. He pulled the covers up a little. I looked at his face, which was emaciated as on the first day. But his eyes had lost that expression of slightly bewildered anxiety which had affected me so much then. The look in the depth of the hollows had become clear and serene. Not reassuring, however, because of this: such calm, such serenity, is also possible when one has reached the depth of final renunciation.

I went out with the doctor.

"In danger? Not if he's properly taken care of. The small bronchia are not affected. A touch of pleurisy at the base of the left lung, but not alarming. Of course we'll take an X-ray by and by, to be on the safe side. What he needs right now is to be kept in bed, to have good care, and to be cautious. Whose house is this? The view here is wonderful."

"It belongs to old Laouëdec, of Cronan. The one who drove you out. He sleeps here sometimes in the winter, so that he can pull up his nets at dawn. Comfortable, certainly . . ."

"Don't let the patient catch cold, that's all. As for the rest . . . Tell me, the sea must be pretty high. Will I be able to get across?"

"We're in a neap tide. You can still get over the bar." I smiled. "This isn't an inaccessible, out-of-the-way island, like mine."

"Ten times more out-of-the-way, to my way of thinking. What difference does it make that it is sometimes joined to the mainland, if the nearest house is leagues away? Besides, with a boat . . ."

We started across the rocky strip. I held the doctor's arm, for he was not too sure-footed.

"I don't care," he said. "Returning from Germany and picking out that . . . that . . . hermitage! You must admit . . ."

"He didn't entirely pick it out. There were circumstances, too."

"You told me he wouldn't leave there."

"It's rather complicated. He doesn't want to put out old Laouëdec by inflicting a sick man on him in his house in Cronan, but he'll go back there as soon as he's cured. Meanwhile he refuses to go anywhere else. That's all."

We walked on in silence. The doctor was not in his element on the rocks.

"Did he catch cold at sea?"

"Yes. When he went with Laouëdec to set out the lobster pots, by the Douvres. They were caught in a squall on the way back, during the night. The waters are treacherous, and they hove to until daylight. They got soaked."

"What's the name of this island?"

"Jews' Island, it seems, but I'm not sure. Old Laouëdec showed it to me one day, before he had rented it. 'It's Jews' Island,' he told me. 'Where the little house is it used to be a convent. A Jew convent. Lucky there ain't no more of 'em there now. I don't like those fellows.' 'A Jewish convent, *père* Laouëdec? Are you sure?' 'Yes,' he said explicitly, 'Jesuits. I don't like 'em.'. . . You can draw your own conclusion, Doctor."

We reached the shore. The coal-burning car was waiting at the end of the road. Old Laouëdec was watching for us anxiously.

"Monsieur Pierre isn't taken too sick, is he?"

"Not too sick. He'd be better off at your house in Cronan, though," said the doctor. "He's stubborn as a mule."

"Can you beat it, can you beat it!" the other exclaimed in a tone of heartbroken anger. "If it isn't a shame! He don't want my old woman getting herself tired out, he says. But I, *sacré bordel* . . ."

"He must eat well," said the doctor.

"Don't you worry about that. I go there every day to pull up my hoop nets. I'll fetch him what he needs."

The doctor had him get into his car, and they disappeared.

∿

The wind was rising. It had passed from the east to the Suroît. Clouds were quickly piling up. I decided it would be prudent to change the anchorage. I climbed aboard and took my little cutter to leeward of the island. I moored it securely, and then proceeded slowly to the old house, amid the brambles and the gorse. The shutters were banging a little. I made them fast and entered the rustic room in which Pierre was resting.

It was a very dark room, in spite of the fact

that the walls were whitewashed. But the nets, the fishing tackle, a whole assortment of spars, oars, rope, pots of tar, moldy old sails, and all kinds of other ill-defined objects cluttered the walls and the floor, consuming the meager light which the single low, narrow window avariciously let through.

"Do you want me to light up?"

"I'm rather low on candles," said Pierre. His bed was in an alcove, and entirely in the shadow. I could barely make out his face against the pillow. "Just leave some matches where I can reach them, I'll light up later on, if necessary. Now run along, before it gets dark."

"Not at all. I'm quite comfortable here."

I was far from sure that he would be pleased. But I wasn't worrying about that.

"You're crazy!" he exclaimed. "What reason is there . . . I'm as strong as an ox. If you think just because of a cold . . . Why did that crazy old Laouëdec have to go and disturb you!"

"Excuse me, but from the way you look it's easy to understand why he might be worried. What's more, we've been looking for you for three days all over the archipelago. Now we've found you. It's saved me a lot of unnecessary trouble."

I spoke without graciousness, I'm afraid.

Pierre remained motionless. His head sank into the pillow.

"I suppose," he finally said without moving, in a noncommittal voice, "that you intend to take care of me, to cure me, and bring me back to the world?"

"I have no intentions whatsoever."

He was motionless. Motionless as a corpse.

"I wouldn't go along with you," he said.

I did not answer. I had sat down on a chair, and I was leaning against the wall.

The silence lasted a very long time. The light faded beyond the window, shaded into gold and into purple. The wind took on volume, moaned in the slate of the roof, sang in the gorse, and the muffled pounding of the tide became audible. That monotonous clamor, too, was part of the silence. The dark room was like a silence within a silence.

Pierre stirred a little — very little. He kept himself from stirring, I could feel. On two or three occasions I heard a nervous little sound, the faint clacking made by the tongue as it separates from the palate. Between times nothing. This lasted a long while. I did not budge. At last — at last — he couldn't stand it and whispered:

"Go away. Please, I'm begging you."

I said, "Don't expect me to."

He lifted his torso, leaned on one elbow, and extended toward me his starved-bird face.

"What do you want?" he burst out in a choked voice.

I said nothing and remained quite motionless. I was in the darkest corner of the room, among the spars, the sails, and the nets. I knew that he could see nothing of me, that he could barely make out where I was sitting.

He let himself fall back on the bed, his head sinking into the hollow of the pillow. He looked altogether like a dead man.

"Can't I be left in peace?" he murmured after a time.

I thought perhaps the moment had come, and I articulated a clear "No."

I waited a little. He did not move. I said:

"Do you think there aren't enough dead already? That France still has too many of her best sons? You won't go along with me, you say, you won't come back to the world. Tell me — what name do you give to this refusal, to this surrender?"

He sighed — he seemed completely exhausted.

"So that's it?"

"Yes," I said, "that's it."

It took him a long time to bring himself to utter the words that followed.

"You think I'm being pretty weak, don't you?" he said in a half whisper.

I did not answer: yet this in itself was an answer, and probably of the worst kind. Pierre said, in a quiet voice:

"And so I am. Only . . ." He seemed to ponder before he went on, "What is one to do when that is what duty commands, when cowardice and honesty go hand in hand?"

I said, "That's an illusion." I hesitated for a moment, then added, "Or a subterfuge."

I had hit the mark. He sat bolt upright on his bed, seemed about to leap from it.

"A subterfuge? How can you dare . . . What do you know that . . ." He calmed himself as suddenly as he had let himself be carried away. "Oh," he said, "naturally, you have a right to think as you do. You have a perfect right."

I felt vexed. He seemed to me to be trying to seize a handful of quicksilver. But I waited: Pierre had let himself fall back, and I felt him to be on the verge of that extreme weariness beyond which all will power finally abdicates and submits.

The inexhaustible clamor outside had become aggravated by new voices. The rain hammered the roof, rolling its R's with a soporific monotony. The surf pounded the rocks with a thundering roar. The wind assaulted the walls with an obsessing patience. My own nerves were suffering from these continually recurring noises; but they made common cause with me — against Pierre. I seemed to feel him slowly, slowly lose his footing, let himself be carried unresistingly by the enveloping tide of fatigue and obedience.

I saw him slowly pass a hand over his face. He uttered a convulsive sigh. Then another, calmer one, which expressed abdication and relief, even more than uncertainty and anguish.

He surrendered.

"What do you want?" he asked feebly.

I took the plunge:

"What happened at Hochswörth?"

He didn't even give a start. Had he foreseen what was to come? Our words fell like a stone at the bottom of a well: the mute, dark water shuts in upon itself — it is stirred, to be sure, by waves that feverishly cross and recross one another, but one can neither see nor hear them.

I waited. My heart was aching.

Pierre spoke in a matter-of-fact voice, so devoid of intonation that it seemed to come from a region even beyond despair:

"I lost my humanity."

⌀

I would not wish on anyone ever to hear such words. I do not know if the sky outside all at once darkened, or if it was an illusion: the shades of night appeared to me in that moment to invade the remotest nooks and crannies of the somber room, already deeply submerged in the twilight gloom. And over there, fused into the heavy obscurity of the alcove, that motionless form, that head buried in the pillow with the macabre weight of death. . . . Perhaps this was why suddenly there came to me the strange thought, "They've killed him . . ."

He said — yes, seeming as it did to rise in a murmur from the heart of darkness, it was indeed a voice from beyond time that is measured in days.

"You know where I've come from. You know,

you think you know. You say: from Hell." I caught a kind of laugh. "Ah, yes, Hell! . . . Fire, brimstone, eternal suffering . . . what is it?"

I had difficulty in hearing him. The wind, the storm . . . yes, that undoubtedly. But most of all my heart. My chest ached. The blood pounded in my ears.

He repeated slowly, in a half voice:

"What is it? Pain, cold, hunger . . . I'll tell you: It's atrocious, but it's bearable. Yes, all you need to do . . . all you need to do is to harden your soul sufficiently. As a diamond is hard, I mean: not letting anything leave a mark on it. A hard-shelled soul is an inviolable refuge." He slowly repeated, in a tone of impersonal observation, "Inviolable." He continued, "I was beaten, bludgeoned, knocked down. With cudgels, with iron rods. Twenty times they left me for dead . . . but never quite let me die, they always stopped in time!" he cried in a voice so charged with resentment and rage that I shuddered. "One can hold out against blows, cudgels, spit," he continued calmly. "It's a matter of finding refuge within yourself. Everyone has his own method. One will recite Virgil to himself. Another prays. I . . ." he stirred a little . . . "I had composed a litany for myself; a euchology, an invocation of the men I admire. Brutus, Louis Blanc, Robespierre . . . the noble Bonchamp, the stubborn Lenin, Pascal, Socrates, Copernicus . . . I would think intently of Richelieu dying a slow, endless death and yet without any weakening carrying on his intense labor . . . of Renoir paralyzed, with his brushes tied to his twisted hands, painting light and the joy of living . . . of Guillaumet, lost in the icy desert of the Andes, frozen, broken, blinded, but in obedience to his family duty walking, walking in the storm and the snow, so that his body would be found. . . . That domain, the frontiers of that domain, no one can encroach on. Oh, one can die that way, to be sure! Thank God, one can die that way. He who dies that way is still a man. . . ."

I heard him stir. The wood of the bed creaked.

"Dying is easy . . . At least," he whispered as if to himself (he sighed), "that is what you think . . . You say to yourself, 'No one can rob me of that freedom. They will never bring me so low that I won't first be able to get off the road.' Only . . ." Suddenly he cried out, in a hoarse voice full of trembling fury, "The dogs! The dogs! Did they know? Did they have that fiendish cunning?" He went on, with bitter haste, "I wonder,

I wonder if I was not as stupidly fooled, as fool-
ishly, as blindly led, trapped, duped as a bull in
the arena. . . . A red rag, *banderillas,* that's all
that is needed . . . the same thing a hundred
times, ten thousand times, and still that's all that
is needed. . . . The animal starts running, charges,
fights, resists, rebels, spends itself, becomes exhausted . . . and suddenly finds itself emptied,
broken, a heavy torpid mass without will, without resilience . . . it has become the property,
the plaything of the *torero.* How, at what moment,
did this happen? At what moment did it lose control of its muscles and its instinct? At what instant,
at what second? When did it cease to be a bull
and become changed into cattle? And we — what
about us? When do we cease to be free beings, beings who can still choose — be able to decide in
favor of death — prefer annihilation to abjectness?
When? At what point of the slope? On what day,
at what hour?"

For some time now the storm had boomed in
the distance. Several times the windowpanes had
paled with vague gleams, still too distant to light
up the room. The flash of a closer streak of lightning illuminated the walls, the ceiling, the alcove.
I held back a cry. That immense, fleshless form, all

white, sitting on the edge of the bed, that death-
like face, that phantom body, a little bent . . .
The moment before I thought of him as lying
down full length with the immobility of a corpse
. . . This unexpected apparition frightened me as
it would an old woman. I also had time to notice
his pale fists, tightly squeezed between his knees.

"The bull's first mistake is to believe in the battle, to believe in the fairness of the contest, to
believe that by keeping himself alive, by retard-
ing his death, he is opposing the enemy's views.
. . . Cruel self-deception! His death matters little.
What matters to his torturers is his degradation,
that he should become that contemptible thing
which is turned into laughingstock. . . . That he
should pass imperceptibly from his nobility of a
brave, proud beast to the abject submission of a
head of cattle. . . . If he had refused the battle
. . . well, he would have been brought back to
the *toril* and led to the slaughterhouse. And then
is when he would have foiled . . . that . . . dia-
bolical . . ."

A fit of coughing interrupted him. He coughed
for a long time, painfully. I should have made him
get back into bed. I did not have the will power. I

136

am not sure if it occurred to me. I was fascinated
and congealed.

"The slaughterhouse is where they take the ordinary animals. They make good butcher meat. Only
the best ones are worth reducing to submission.
I did not realize that Hochswörth was both a
slaughterhouse and a circus. They waved the red
rag, they stuck *banderillas* into hides: it did not
take long to make the selection. The slaughterhouse functioned day and night, but not for us.
Not for us!" he exclaimed with such a note of despair that I felt an impulse to stop up my ears. "Oh,
blind that I was, proud and wretched blind man!
Didn't I know it since the first day, since the time
when I foiled their fiendish schemes by jumping
out of the window? Didn't I know that they must
have witnesses, ever more witnesses for their in-
famous victory? For the atrocious victory of contempt, the abominable science which has contempt
as an end and man as a means? A dreadful, but
fragile victory, unceasingly challenged. And so,
didn't I know that they must unceasingly, never
sufficiently unceasingly, unceasingly, and unceasingly prove to themselves that man is contemptible? Now what proof could be more probing than

the degradation of a noble creature to the last degree of abjection? I knew it, I knew it! And yet I played into their hands. I believed, wretched idiot that I was, that I could beat them at their own game. I did not understand the paralyzing trick of the red rag and the *banderillas*. I fought, stood my ground, resisted, I was not willing to make them the servile gift of my death. I thought, 'I'm still on my feet. Later on. I have time.' I did not feel my strength weaken, when already I had lost it. . . ."

A heavy heat had invaded the room. I felt oppressed and damp. The lightning fell not far away, and the rain on the roof came down in great sheets. It seemed to relieve me.

"From every ordeal," Pierre went on, "from every ordeal I thought I had come out the winner. The beatings, the endless roll calls in the snow and the icy wind, the awful weariness from carrying heavy loads that served no purpose — as I told you, I recited my litanies to myself, and I never flinched. The latrines where we had to stand up to our bellies and which we had to clean out with our bare hands, after having been ordered to squat in them in obscene and grotesque squads in front of the women on the other side of the barbed wires; those degrading tasks, those imposed marks

138

of debasement, all those things remained external and did not touch me. Hunger, progressive atrophy, exhaustion — they make you want to die, that's all. Death . . . we lived with it. What can death, sooner or later, do to you when it is your everyday companion? I went five times to the gas chamber. Five times," he repeated slowly to make me thoroughly understand what that meant. "They would make us get up, at midnight. They gave us a piece of soap, and a towel, according to the ritual, and it had become so little of a deception that at last we laughed about it. . . . Yes, we would joke about it: after a certain point is reached it becomes strangely simple to trifle, to laugh about your own end. They stripped our poor bodies. And we would go and stand in line. Stand in line, yes, in order to enter the death shop where peace and sleep would at last be dispensed us. . . . One batch would enter. Then another. We would await our turn to die. And then the door would be shut in our faces. We would have to dress again, fumbling for our clothes in the dark, and go back to our barracks. We would wake up from our death agony. Until the next time." In a strangely natural tone he repeated, "They killed me five times in eight months."

The storm was now altogether upon us. A series of thunderclaps accompanied by intense flickering lightning strokes filled my ears and eyes. I saw that Pierre was upright. In his white pajamas, too big for his emaciated carcass, he looked like a consumptive, wretched Pierrot. He was pacing in his alcove as he must have paced the floor of his cell in the prison of Fresnes: three steps, back and forth, like a lion in a cage. The lightning flashed on him intermittently, immobilizing him for a second before my eyes like a snapshot, and gave to his long, atrophied members the baroque and alarming attitudes of a skeleton.

"The last time . . ." he said, and it seemed to me that his voice was trembling, "it was . . . some time . . . only a few weeks before the camp was liberated. We knew perfectly well that the end was approaching . . . not so soon, though . . . and in any case . . . that we should be left alive was such an absurd hypothesis . . ." He broke off and coughed. I don't know why his cough did not strike me as very natural — as though he were trying to gain time. ". . . It was the last queue, the final liquidation; it seemed to me . . . seemed to me so obvious . . . It was longer than ever and it had been started early. This time at last I was not

far from the door. For nine days we had eaten
nothing. Nothing at all. And drunk only what we
could find in filthy ditch holes. There we were,
naked and shivering, soiled, hideous to look upon,
standing on our shaky pins, God knows how. There
were all kinds of people this time among us, not
only those who, like myself . . . It was a big batch,
there were all kinds of wailing and weeping. A
really rather . . . rather . . . ignoble sight. I was
as if in a dream, I had reached that point . . .
that point of . . . mental dissolution . . . where
I could not even bring myself to have a feeling of
. . . regret . . . or of relief . . . Nothing. Not
even impatience or fear. Nothing, emptiness. A
head of cattle, a head of cattle at the gates of the
slaughterhouse. Did I realize it? I no longer know.
Perhaps there remained . . . yes, something like
a shadow, a ghost of . . . of satisfaction, of
pride . . ." he uttered a brief sneer . . ."of grat-
ification, let's say, at having reached the end without having succumbed. Not once in thirteen
months, not once in spite of the floggings and the
threats of death, had I yielded, had I been willing
to . . . touch a single hair of a comrade. Ten
times I had been left more than half-dead on the
ground after . . . after such refusals. Now I was

going to die, and I was glad. 'Death, where is thy victory?' I was not beaten.

"Did I think all this out clearly? No, certainly not . . . It was like . . . a deposit at the bottom of a bottle that has been left standing too long . . . if you shake the bottle it comes to the surface, otherwise it remains unnoticed but . . . you know it's there. That's all. That was all. I was waiting and my head was empty. . . . What I was seeing appeared to me . . . like a nightmare, but like someone else's nightmare, a nightmare that doesn't concern you. The Nazis themselves called us NN's — *Nacht und Nebel:* Night and Fog. . . . We were standing in line along a dirty wall, and on the other side . . . the other wall . . . were the furnaces. They were lighted and were roaring away. A familiar sight, to me. It was the fifth time, you know. I no longer looked — even looked. Every moment prisoners, pushing handcarts full of corpses, came and unloaded them. Natural deaths — that is to say, typhus, tuberculosis, starvation . . . They were piling up.

"Then . . . I saw the tall SS, right next to me. He said, 'You.' I didn't catch on right away, didn't understand. Someone nudged me — one of my fellow prisoners in the line. The SS seized me by the shoulder and with a blow sent me a good ten paces, toward the furnaces. Then he came, without hurrying. He showed me the pile of corpses, the poor pile of human carrion. 'Put those in the furnace.'

"No, I thought to myself (but very feebly). That or something else . . . the body, you understand . . . the husk . . . back there you quickly learn to consider it for what it is: a mass of rotting cells. 'The spirit is refined through suffering' — above all it becomes the only thing that counts. Quite the only thing. The only thing worthy of respect and love. It's a hundred times better that this poor suffering shell when the spirit has left should turn to ashes, than to dissolve into refuse and stench. . . . I picked up in my arms the first of these pitiful anatomies, so emaciated, so shriveled, so grotesquely twisted and deformed that I hardly thought I was lifting a human body . . . and yet . . . did my poor carcass in its repulsive nakedness look any better? Oh, so little. . . . One dead man lifting another dead man. . . . I lifted him with difficulty, puffing and panting, for the least effort exhausted me. I threw him as best I could on a kind of cart which in a single movement tips and throws its load into the open mouth of the furnace. . . . And it was then . . . when he was there, on his back . . . that I saw . . .

"I knew his face: how could I have forgotten it? For more than a month we had been chained to the same hell. The two of us trundled a kind of barrow loaded with rocks. Without letup we had to pass along the same way between two sheds. At the corner of one of these a jailer waited for us, a boy of fifteen or sixteen, day after day. And there, without ever varying, he would bring down his club on the skull of whichever of us was in the lead. Each trip we would trade places, so as to receive an equal number of blows. . . . Poor fellow, so he had died before me. I looked at his wretched face, beside which mine would seem fat to you. And then . . ."

He shied, like a horse before an obstacle. The effort which he made was so evident that I could almost feel the sharp point of the spur. He continued in a voice without resonance, trembling and muffled:

"Then he opened his eyes. The lids slowly lifted on his dim eyes, pale, colorless eyes. Yes. And he looked at me. He saw me. He moved one hand a little and even . . . ah . . . he tried, he succeeded . . . he opened his lips in a ghost of a smile. It was horrible and prodigious, horrible and staggering, but for me it was only horrible, horrible, most horrible. I took a step backward and turned round. The tall SS was there, with his hands in his pockets, his club under his arm. He was smiling. He said, 'Well?'

"I said nothing. I tried to pass between the cart and him, to get back into the line, to wait for death in my place, at the door to the gas chamber. He caught me by the forearm and threw me against the furnace. It was burning hot and I could not keep from screaming. My shoulder was all burnt. The tall SS held me at a distance with the end of his club. He said to me, 'Throw him in the fire. Right away. Or else . . .' He looked at me a moment with pitiless, mocking eyes, and he was pushing me toward the fire, toward the red-hot, roaring fire. '. . . Or else you go into the fire yourself.' As I didn't seem to understand, he turned round. 'You, there!' he shouted, 'and you!' And I saw the faces of the two men in the line, two poor creatures half reverted to a stage of savagery, I saw their faces light up with an ignominious hope. . . . They took a step. I was more . . . I was weaker than I thought. My poor stumps failed me. I fell. Ah, they had a way of getting you up again with a club, even if you were a corpse! 'Stick him in the furnace, right away,' he yelled, 'or else . . .' He kept me pinned to the cart, digging his club into my side. I was too close to the door of the furnace; in there the flames roared and whirled, and even at this distance the heat was awful. The SS said, 'No?' He made a sign to the two men, who began to lift their arms, like two gorillas . . . The furnace was searing my back . . . they began advancing, at first slowly, because they weren't very sure . . . The SS was laughing . . . I saw them run . . .

"There," he said in a voice so low (a mere breath) and so strangely calm that it gave me gooseflesh. "I found myself holding the empty cart. . . . The long cry, the horrible cry was silenced, and in the fire the body was burning, bubbling, sizzling, and I began to smell it. The SS said, 'All right . . . the next one.' And I put in the next one. He was dead, I think, quite dead. But that was just by chance. The others, too, were dead — but what difference does that make . . ." he exclaimed in a kind of yelp into which his voice strangled — and he continued to cry in a broken, husky, feverish pitch . . . "when in order to save yourself you have thrown a man into a blazing furnace, a liv-

ing man, a friend, a comrade, with his eyes looking at you and a smile . . . and a smile . . . a
smile . . . a . . ."

May God spare me from ever hearing again the
strange gargling sound which choked the end of
these words. An intolerable garble of sobs, phrases
without sequel, inarticulate words. I heard, "Oh
. . . oh . . . oh . . ." and in a gleam, in the already distant light of the storm which was fleeing
in the direction of the Anglo-Norman islands, I
saw that he had buried his face in the pillow and
was turning it from side to side, as a child does in
the throes of despair.

And I, in my corner, amid the nets and the
ropes and the old broken spars, had also given way
to the weakness of tears. They flowed silently, and
I did not wipe them away, I did not even attempt
to hold them back. For I was horrified by the feelings I was experiencing: above pity, above the
brotherly tenderness which such a cruel, such an
outrageously undeserved misfortune inspired in
me, I felt rising the intolerable sensation of a
nausea and a repugnance against which I struggled
in vain. An irrational repulsion like that which
came over me one day when a friend, having put
into my hands a book with a strange binding, sud-

denly said to me, "It's made of human skin. . . ."
My feeling this evening was so odiously unjust that
I should have liked to take it upon myself to get
up, to go over and put my arms around that poor
stricken form and embrace it — but I could not
bring myself to do this. And then I thought of
Nicole — of Pierre and Nicole, of their love. And
I understood.

"Forgive me," I heard suddenly. "This weakness
is unworthy, isn't it, of . . . My nerves aren't very
steady yet . . . Please take that into account.

"Now you know the worst. I continued this oc-
cupation for seven weeks. I put bodies into the
furnaces by the hundreds — perhaps by the thousands. They were generally dead, but probably not
all. I didn't check. It was a matter of utter and
complete indifference to me. Sometimes after a
series of stiff and icy corpses I would hold in my
arms a body that was still warm with a remnant
of life. What difference did it make? One or ten
thousand, what difference did it make? It was too
late." He repeated slowly, with bitterness, "Too
late . . ." and once again, with hardness and em-
phasis, as though he were speaking to some person
whom he wished to chastise, "Too late." And he
went on in a voice that was very slow, very low

and veiled, "Do you un-der-stand? There are . . . there are dreadful gestures, gestures from which there is no appeal . . . which all the perfumes of sweet Araby . . . One has made the gesture and . . . too late. Forever too late."

He was silent and I listened to him for a long time breathing with effort; he breathed calmly but with effort — as one sometimes hears, at the end of a dark room, a sleeper haunted by a painful dream.

"During all that time I was not even unhappy," he finally continued, and his voice struck me as tinged with an unendurable irony. "I was so sure . . . it was so obvious that this was but an absurd postponement of my own death. Before my own body should in turn pass through the gaping mouth of the furnace was only a question of days — a question which depended solely on the humor of the jailers. Meanwhile this employment afforded me a less wretched life: I slept on a straw bed, I could wash, my hair began to grow again, and at mealtimes I was brought things which bore some resemblance to food. . . . Yes, and I accepted this additional degradation. I didn't care. I didn't care, I didn't care," he repeated as though he were cracking nuts between his teeth. "In the end I caught typhus. It seems that I keeled over one night, next to the cart which I had just unloaded. . . . Why wasn't I thrown in, as I should have been — as I had a right to expect? Perhaps because . . . we had been hearing the sound of guns for the last two or three days . . . the Americans were approaching . . . perhaps that was why . . . in the confusion and the panic . . . in any case I found myself in the hospital one day. Saved." It was painful to hear him repeat with a laugh, "Saved . . . !" He said bitterly, "There you are . . . I was brought to life." He gave a long sigh and murmured, each word uttered in a half whisper with an accent of anger or despair, "I have been brought back among men."

He was silent. And after a very long interval he said:

"That's all. Now, please, leave me alone. Go away."

I got up. I was hesitant and uncertain. What could I have said? I look a few steps toward the door. I remained there, motionless and full of indecision, with my hand on the knob. Did he think I had left? I heard him murmur:

"So many years still before me. So many years . . ."

It was not addressed to me, nor to anyone. To the gods perhaps. I opened the door.

A last gleam revealed him to me as he lay, curled up a little, under the sheet, with his head toward the wall. I went out.

The night was very dark. The moon seemed to leap from cloud to cloud, hurrying toward the earth. As I went down I struck my foot against the point of a rock and hurt myself. I got into my little cutter in the calm of its sheltered cove, and lay down fully dressed in the cabin. I spent the last hours of the night falling asleep and waking up twenty times. Like Hamlet, I had heard from a specter the story of the blackest crime that can be conceived: the murder of a soul.

Murder most foul, as in the best it is;
But this most foul, strange and unnatural . . .

Everything can be forgiven — perhaps even murder. But a soul! . . .

When dawn broke I could stand it no longer and went back up toward the silent house, and the mute hell which it contained between its walls.

Pierre was sleeping in the same attitude in which I had left him. The sheet rose and fell rhythmically, outlining his thin shoulder.

I stood there a long time, my heart rent with anguish.

I went down again to the cutter and set sail. The wind was due north and enabled me to make my way back against the ebb tide.

When I got home I buried myself in an arm-chair. And since then I have been questioning myself.

In vain, as may be suspected. What can one do against the implacable feeling that Pierre expressed by those words, "I have lost my humanity"? Who could help him to win it back — if not himself? What can one hope for?

I don't know.

I don't know, I don't know.

The Verdun Press

A TRANSLATION BY HAAKON M. CHEVALIER

OF *L'Imprimerie de Verdun*

BY VERCORS

THE VERDUN PRESS

DOWN WITH the thieves!"

It was a vindictive cry, and Vendresse poured out his whole heart in giving vent to it on that deceptively mild February day. He meant it. He hated thieves. "They're the ones who got us into this."

I liked Vendresse. He was fervent and sincere. His sincerity, his fervor, just took the wrong road, that was all. He called me a Bolshevik, half jokingly — but only half jokingly. He knew I was not a member of "the party," that I would never be a member of a party. But I did not belong to his either: the only party which he considered honest, the only one inspired by love of order and of "*la patrie*." He did not like the "fellows of the Action Française" any better, who were just as

subversive in their way. Oh, he was all for a social
upheaval, too, but for an ordered kind of upheaval,
an upheaval directed against the thieves.

"But where are these thieves that you keep talking about?" I said.

"Well, of all things!" he exploded, looking at
me round-eyed.

I pressed my advantage. "You should read what
a friend of mine wrote the other day — 'Why not
shout "Down with the murderers!" to the *Gare
de l'Est*,' he suggested, 'and burn up the old
wooden railroad coaches which kill two hundred
passengers at a time, because insurance on them
cost the company less than on new coaches?' "

"Oh," Vendresse protested, "coaches that can
still be used!"

That was my Vendresse for you, and I looked
with amusement at his little printing press all
cluttered with useless objects — old plates, old
wrenches, old advertising ash trays, old nuts, and
even an old pressure gauge from heaven knows
what boiler — which he couldn't bring himself to
throw away ("I might find some use for them").

Verdun Press. The name was rather startling
above the narrow shop, set into an angle of the
Passage d'Enfer — Hell Passage — in Montparnasse.

Why Verdun? The hell of Verdun? one wondered. That could be read into it, to be sure, though the connection was not deliberate. Vendresse had been half-apprentice, half-journeyman in 1914 when the war broke out. After his employer left, he kept the establishment open until he himself was called, at the end of 1915. Both were wounded at Verdun — in different regiments. Vendresse made a good recovery. But the boss had to have his right foot amputated: gangrene had set in. A little later the operation had to be repeated, above the knee. Then his whole thigh followed, and finally it passed into his left leg. When he went on the operating table for the sixth time (the other thigh), he mentioned Vendresse in his will and left him the printing press — in memory of Verdun.

That was how Vendresse, in 1924, became his own boss and baptized the printing shop with that glorious name. Oh, it was a modest enterprise: only job work — social announcements, letterheads, folders. . . . An automatic Minerva, a pedal press, and a funny old hand press. It was for the last of these that I used to come, to collect proofs for books I was publishing.

A small employer, but an employer nevertheless.

He set great store by this status. This was undoubtedly why he had gone and shouted, "Down
with the thieves!" in protest against the taxes.
Which are too heavy because the Jews wax fat, the
freemasons rob, and the "Bolsheviks" commit
sabotage.

He made a great distinction between these di-
verse entities and the individuals who constitute
them. Thus his journeyman was a Jew, a freemason,
and an antifascist. This triple blemish did not
prevent Vendresse from esteeming him highly.
"Some of them are all right," he said. This journeyman was a little chap from Briançon, ardent,
lively, hard-working and skillful, who had also
been through Verdun. After the war he had bought
from a cousin of his a small printing press in the
Piedmont region, in Pignerolle. Fascism had chased
him out. Vendresse had hired him — again in
memory of Verdun. Dacosta and he quarreled violently three times a week over Mussolini. After
which they would go and have a beer on Rue
Campagne-Première. They were crazy about each
other.

Things nearly took a bad turn in '36. Dacosta
felt obliged to go on strike, out of solidarity. He
notified his boss, assuring him that he would work

additional hours the following weeks, to make up for it, at the same wage. Vendresse stormed and fumed, and threatened to fire him. "If there was an employers' strike," said Dacosta, "you would join it, wouldn't you? Even if I threatened to leave." Vendresse continued to shout, for form's sake. But the argument hit home. He was sensitive to justice.

The Munich crisis was very acute at the printing press. "It's shameful, shameful," Dacosta would say, and his narrow mouth would quiver under the little mustache, and his black eyes become clouded with tears. "Come, come," Vendresse would say, "let's be fair: if the Czechs have been mistreating those Sudetens, after all! Hitler is doing the right thing."

"What about the Jews, aren't they being mistreated in Germany? Who's doing anything for them?" said Dacosta with suppressed rage.

"I don't know about that," said Vendresse. "That's a lot of communist propaganda."

"And what about the Sudetens — isn't that propaganda? I'm telling you, *patron:* in making concession after concession as we're doing it's easy to see the way we're headed. In three years we'll be enslaved."

"Enslaved!" Vendresse thundered. "Enslaved! Aren't we already enslaved? By the Jews and the freemasons?"

There followed a painful silence. The employee, a Jew and a freemason, looked at his employer with a gentle irony. . . . And Vendresse felt rather foolish, rummaged in his pockets to find a pipe which he knew to be somewhere else, adjusted his little round glasses on his little bit of a red nose, moved his thick lips under the mustache stained red by cigarettes.

The war came. Vendresse and Dacosta had both passed the forty mark. They were mobilized in the labor companies. I knew some people in the Premier Bureau: Vendresse asked me to intercede and, in April, 1940, they were reunited. Their company worked in the forest of Compiègne. Dacosta was a sergeant, and Vendresse just a private: they thought that was funny.

When in June the Fritzes were threatening Compiègne, the company was assigned to fell some trees across the road between the St.-Ouen Cross and Verberie. Toward evening they began to hear the armored convoys on the right bank of the Oise, and also in the forest on Highway 332, while the aviation pounded the Vaudrepont crossroads.

They hastened back to their quarters in St. Sauveur, where they found that there was no one left: the captain had made off in his Citroën with the two lieutenants.

"The bastards," said Dacosta. "That's your elite for you," he said to Vendresse. "The insurance lawyer, the liquor dealer, and the little whippersnapper in the regular army. Fine patriots!"

"Mustn't generalize," said Vendresse irritably. "And besides, maybe they had orders."

In any case, Dacosta took command of the abandoned company and undertook to effect its retreat. They escaped the *Panzers* by a hairsbreadth in Senlis, were overtaken at Dammartin, disengaged themselves under cover of darkness, crossed the Marne at the Trilbardou dam, and definitely broke away at Pithiviers. Aside from a few stragglers, oldsters of forty-eight who let themselves be caught, when they slumped with exhaustion into a ditch, Dacosta brought his company intact as far as Gien. They suffered some losses during the crossing of the Loire; a group in the second platoon, under the command of a disheartened old private, gave up during the night between Bourges and Montluçon; nevertheless when they finally reached Clermont, on their last legs, Dacosta still had under control more than two thirds of his unit. He received an army citation. General G—— publicly congratulated him.

Pétain seized power. "At last!" said Vendresse.

"Well," said Dacosta, "*you're* not scared."

"Of what?" Vendresse barked. "Nobody but he can get us out of this mess. If he'd been called in sooner . . . Pétain: Verdun. What are you scared of?"

"The Republic is *Kaputt,*" said Dacosta. "And as for us Jews, it's going to go hard."

Vendresse burst out laughing. "You know, frankly, as far as I'm concerned the Jews can go to hell, but fellows like you . . . Verdun and your decorations . . . do you think for one minute the Old Man would let his *poilus* down? You're a fine son of a bitch."

They were demobilized on August 3. A train was made up, that very evening, for the liberated Parisians. Those who wanted to go back had to make up their minds immediately: the Germans, they were told, would not allow individual returns thereafter. For Dacosta it was an agonizing decision to make: was he going to let himself into the clutches of the Krauts? "With my name they're just as likely to pick me up before I get any further than Moulins."

"What are you talking about?" said Vendresse. "They don't give a damn. Don't worry, I'm telling you. You've got nothing to be afraid of with the Old Man. No nonsense. You're coming back with me."

He went back.

The press was reopened, and little by little the work resumed. All went well, except that relations between the boss and his employee were becoming a little strained. Vendresse exulted. "What did I tell you, eh? The Old Man. Even here the Fritzes don't dare to do anything."

"Go east, and up north," said Dacosta, "and see what they're doing."

"That's a lot of talk," said Vendresse.

And the discussion would turn bitter.

Toward the end of January Vendresse received a visit. It was a colleague — well, an electroprinter. His card bore the inscription, *Member of the Veterans' Association of Printers, Engravers, and Binders. — Member of* L'AMICALE DES VIEUX DE VERDUN. His name was Paars. He was fat, a little too elegantly dressed. His plump, rather soft cheeks, smooth-shaven, were blotched under the powder. They first spoke about the weather, as is proper, in order to get acquainted. Then:

"So, you fought at Verdun, too?" said Vendresse.

"And how," said Paars.

"What sector?"

"Well . . . in Verdun, right in the town. In the transfer units." He winked. "A cushy job."

"Ah, yes . . ."

There was a silence. "And what brings you here?" said Vendresse.

"Well, it's like this," said Paars. "Some of us Veterans of Verdun feel that the moment has come to get rid of the Jews in the profession. We're going to send a petition to Vichy. You'll go along with us, of course?"

Vendresse did not answer immediately. He rummaged in his pockets, looking for a pipe which was somewhere else. He moved some old nuts, some old wrenches, the old pressure gauge, as though this were a matter of great urgency. He finally said, without turning round:

"I go along with the Marshal. I think it's not up to us to tell him what's got to be done; it's up to him to tell us, up to us to do what he says. That's what I think."

He turned round, went behind his desk, sat down. His thick lips moved under the reddened mustache. He coughed.

"And so," he said at last, "how are things in the electropress — going pretty good?"

"Well," said Paars, "I haven't had my shop, you know, since '38. The underhand work of a Jew, as you might expect. But" — he winked his eye — "it won't bring him any luck. . . . All right," he said, getting up, "that's agreed, eh? I'll put down your name."

"Wait a minute, wait a minute," said Vendresse. "Of course I say to hell with the Jews. Only . . ."

He removed his glasses and wiped them. His eyes were tiny without the glasses. He put them on again.

"There are Jews in l'Amicale; I know some. It bothers me."

"If they were in the battle," said Paars with a kind of laugh that quavered between the edges of a contemptuous grimace, "it's because they couldn't help themselves. No use being sentimental, old man."

"Yes, yes, to be sure," said Vendresse. "Just the same, I'd rather wait. The Marshal . . ."

"What do you mean, the Marshal? Ah yes, his

being supposed to have said, 'There were Jews in Verdun.' . . . You make me laugh: do you let your customers know when you're going to put a fast one over on them? Come on, make up your mind: are you giving your name, or aren't you?"

"No, you see, I'm not," said Vendresse.

"All right," said Paars. "I can't force you. You think it over. I had no idea you liked the smell of Jews."

"I don't like their smell," Vendresse retorted with an air of irritation, then added in a calmer, somewhat hesitant voice, "but it bothers me too . . . The day when Pétain tells us . . ."

"You can be easy on that score: you won't have long to wait."

Paars exchanged a few more words with Vendresse, just to preserve appearances, and then he left.

Vendresse circled aimlessly about in his little office for a long time. Before he finally went back into the shop he cast a last glance at the colored portrait of the Marshal in the middle of the wall. "I hate lies . . ."

He went in and looked at Dacosta, who was running off some announcements on the pedal press.

He continued to circle aimlessly about in the shop, rummaging in his pockets in search of a mythical pipe. His thick lips moved. He cast sidelong glances at Dacosta.

In the end he said nothing.

∾

Dacosta had got married a short time before the war. He had a son going on three and a daughter aged twenty months.

They lived in a trim little dwelling, clean and sunny, overlooking the Montparnasse cemetery, on the Rue Froideveaux. On Sundays they liked to have Vendresse over for lunch. In front of the window there was a small terrace, covered in sheet metal, with an iron guardrail. Vendresse and Dacosta, when the weather was good, would take their coffee there. They agreed in thinking that there was nothing particularly sad about a cemetery.

One Sunday at about eleven, Vendresse was shaving before setting out, when the doorbell rang. It was Paars. Oh, Vendresse mustn't interrupt what he was doing, but go right ahead and finish shaving — Paars just happened to pass by, and had dropped in for a chat.

Paars settled his big buttocks into the small

leather armchair, from which the horsehair was coming out a little on one side. He didn't seem to know quite where to put his big arms. His blotched jowls bulged over the starched collar trimly adorned with a bow tie. He had rather queer eyes, imperfectly set between the eyelids, like those of a sandab.

"So," he said laughing, "still a Jew lover?"

Vendresse, under the lather, emitted a sound that might have been a grunt or a laugh.

"You've seen, haven't you, about the Marshal?" Paars went on. "What did I tell you, eh? You've seen the Vichy laws?"

"Pétain can't always do what he wants," said Vendresse. "It seems he said he didn't approve those laws."

"Balls," said Paars. "Look at that: you recognize it?"

He pushed forward his lapel. Vendresse recognized the Frankish battle-ax.

"Not everybody gets that," said Paars.

"You're in with the big shots?" said Vendresse.

"I'm in a bit. I'm with the copper allocation. Grandet got me in there. You know him? No? You could have: he was a bigwig in the Vieux de Verdun and also in Deloncle's league: you know" —

he laughed — "the synarchy, the *cagoulards,* as they call them. . . . He spoke of me to the Marshal. It's true that I'm well posted on the situation in the printing field — from the political point of view, you know what I mean. And then Grandet carries on big-scale operations in copper, and I can lend him a hand. In short, I saw your Marshal. Grandet had told him I had ideas on the subject of the decentralization of big business in the industry. . . . I talked to him about the Jews, so you see . . . I said, 'They've got to be broken.' He said, 'You're the judge as to what has to be done in your field.' I said, 'There's a rumor, Monsieur le Maréchal, that you are rather protecting them, because of those who are veterans.' He smiled — the way he does, you know, with one eye that blinks a little. And he said, 'I have to consider the feelings of the public. Everyone in France does not think in the same way. I can't say unreservedly what I think. My position is very difficult.' He put his hand on my shoulder — yes, my dear fellow. Like an old friend. And he said, 'Always act for the good of the country. And you will always have me behind you!' Now you see! So, if you had any scruples . . ."

"But look here, old man," said Vendresse, "to

my way of thinking, that doesn't mean anything at all! And one might even believe . . . it might even be claimed . . . In other words he encouraged you without encouraging you by encouraging you. That's not open and aboveboard."

"Well, what do you want?"

"I want more than that. That can mean anything, what he told you."

"In any case," said Paars brusquely and almost with a degree of violence, "he did tell me in so many words, 'You're the judge in your field.' So . . ."

He accompanied the last word with a little movement of his hand, short and cutting.

He pulled two cigars from his vest pocket, offered one to Vendresse. While they were lighting them a kind of good-natured smile broadened Paars's face even more.

"I wanted to talk to you about something else, too. There's a boy I'm interested in . . . A young fellow of sixteen. He's just out of school. He's the son of a . . . oh, I'll explain to you some other time. A little stenographer I used to have, at the time of . . . Anyway she had this kid, I'd like to provide for his future. And I thought . . ."

He flicked off with his forefinger a bit of ash

that had fallen on his coat. He scratched the material with absorption. "I thought if he came in with you, it would be exactly the thing for him. All the more as . . ."

He offered Vendresse his broad, good-natured smile.

"You're a bachelor, you'll certainly be retiring one of these days. You can see how nicely it would work out."

Vendresse pulled off his glasses, wiped them, put them back on his little bit of a pink nose.

"Yes, yes, I understand," he said. "Only . . ."

He got up, went to the other end of the room in quest of an advertising ash tray, brought it to the table between them, shook the end of his cigar into it.

"You probably know that I'm not alone?"

"Of course, of course," said Paars.

He gently caressed his jowls, which were streaked with powder over the tiny purple veins.

"This Dacosta fellow," he said, "is a Jew, isn't he?"

"No, not at all," said Vendresse.

He spoke calmly. Ensconced in the depth of his armchair he remained quite motionless, taking slow puffs from his cigar.

"With that name? That's funny," said Paars, "I was sure . . . And wasn't . . . wasn't he banished from Italy once?"

"Yes, a long time ago. But that's his business. Here his conduct has been irreproachable. I'm very satisfied with him."

"All right, all right, too bad," said Paars.

He took two or three puffs without speaking.

"Too bad, too bad," he repeated. "It's a pity. And it bothers me. It's a little difficult to find the boy a good place, he's somewhat backward in certain things. And there is his mother who . . . Yes, a little business like yours would be just right for him. Let's say no more about it. Since you like your Dacosta."

He crushed the butt of his cigar in the ash tray and added, smiling:

"You know what you're doing, don't you?"

Vendresse smiled too, and squarely met the disquieting look in the sandab eyes.

∾

He arrived a little late at Rue Froideveaux. He was not very talkative while Madame Dacosta shared her attentions between the table of the grownups and the babies' requirements. Vendresse kept looking at her every so often. Her delicate face with the timidly smiling lips, the deep, intense black eyes, always a little moist, had stirred in him a fatherly tenderness ever since he could remember. Today that face seemed to him more fragile than ever.

After lunch Madame Dacosta left the two men alone on the little zinc-floored terrace. They smoked in silence. A faint autumnal mist suffused the cemetery with a sun-bathed melancholy. Dacosta looked at his employer, who looked at the smoke of his cigarette. Madame Dacosta came and served the coffee. She left again. They drank in silence. Dacosta rolled a cigarette. Vendresse stuffed his pipe diligently.

"There are some fine sons of bitches on this earth," he said at last.

"That . . ." said Dacosta, and he added nothing more.

Vendresse lit his pipe, took many puffs to get it started.

"I saw one this morning," he said, "he's a corker."

"Ah," said Dacosta.

"All the more a son of a bitch . . ." Vendresse

began, but he saw that Dacosta was looking at him with an expression that might be slightly mocking, and he did not finish.

And then Madame Dacosta came back. She sat down with them. The conversation started up again among the three of them, a little halting.

ᢙᢙ

On the days that followed, Vendresse talked very little. He did a good deal of aimless moving about, straightening things. The work suffered. Dacosta didn't notice it, or pretended not to.

On the Monday of the following week, at about ten o'clock, Vendresse brusquely put on his hat and went over to see a fellow printer on Rue d'Alésia. They spoke of one thing and another, and then Vendresse said:

"Why did they arrest Whemer?"

"Oh," said the other, "you've got a pretty good idea."

Vendresse blushed.

"Yes, yes, of course . . . But tell me just the same."

He didn't like this fellow Whemer. He represented a small firm specializing in paper used for announcements. No particular age. Rather mangy.

"He wasn't wearing the star. He had scratched out his card."

"Was it the Fritzes who nabbed him?" said Vendresse.

"Nothing of the kind."

"Frenchmen?"

"Of course. Besides, he had built up a good trade. There's always somebody who can profit by it. It's natural enough, what do you expect? They were swarming like flies, all those Polacks. I know you don't have much use for them either."

"No," said Vendresse. "But that makes no difference. It's rotten just the same."

He returned to the Passage d'Enfer. On the way he stopped once more on Boulevard Raspail, in front of the red poster bordered with black which he knew well, on which were listed the names of ten communists and as many Jews, shot as hostages.

Dacosta was at his case, composing a public notice (and was grumbling a little because it had to do with a meeting for the benefit of prisoners, under the aegis of the Marshal. They had quarreled on the subject that morning). Vendresse slowly removed his hat, his overcoat, and came toward him

175

with his hands in his pockets, swinging on his little legs. He coughed.

"I say . . ."

Dacosta raised his eyes, looked at the kindly, plump face on which distress and uncertainty were touchingly written. He smiled and said:

"So this is it? I've got to beat it?"

Vendresse was struck speechless. He opened his mouth, raised one hand, said nothing. Dacosta calmly resumed his work.

"If you think," he said, "that I didn't guess what's cooking . . . Didn't I know, from the first day, that we would come to this? It's you, with your Pétain. . . ."

"Never mind Pétain," said Vendresse. "He's got nothing to do with it. It's not his fault if some dirty . . ."

"We're not going to quarrel once more on account of that old crab," said Dacosta. "If I understand correctly, the climate here has become unhealthy for me?"

"I'm afraid so. That big hog Paars is a vile son of a bitch. I was a sap. I persuaded you not to put yourself down as a Jew, and now . . ."

"Don't worry about that. I wouldn't be any bet-

ter off. We'll all get it, I'm telling you — sooner
or later. Maybe it's better that I should be in
trouble now; later it might have been worse."

"Paars wants your job for a half-wit whom he
had by his stenographer, whom he's not anxious
to acknowledge as his own and doesn't know what
to do with because nobody wants a good-for-noth-
ing. I even gathered that he intends to take the
shop off my hands, by hook or by crook, at a soft
price, after I've worn myself out teaching his nin-
compoop the trade. It all comes from my having
kept you with me in violation of the law. He's got
us."

"So what do we do? Do we close?"

"No," said Vendresse. "If I close, Paars will take
over the shop. He's not going to get it while I'm
still alive. You're going to beat it. I'll manage here
without you as long as necessary. Leave your things,
as if you had just stepped out. I'm going to tell
you something, old man: this shop is going to you
— to you and to your son. Never mind the Fritzes
and the Jews."

Dacosta took him in his arms and embraced him.
He said:

"It's too bad, though . . ."

"What?"

"That you're such a decent chap and that you're so easily taken in."

"By whom?"

"By those hypocrites. And to begin with by the hypocrite in chief whom I won't name so as not to spoil this lovely moment. Because it is a lovely moment. Perhaps the last. Well," he said, "I'm at least going to finish this plate. Then I'll pack up my things."

He turned back to his case. Vendresse said:

"Let's see your card."

"My card?"

"Yes; your identity card."

Dacosta handed it to him. Vendresse looked at it and said:

"You need another one. You'll have trouble with this one, even in the free zone."

Dacosta waited. There was a smile all ready on his lips, but he held it back.

"It disgusts me to do this, I hate it," said Vendresse, "but I'll have to make you one. Yes, it disgusts me, it disgusts me. If it weren't for that bastard Paars . . ."

He fumbled around in the case rack to find the characters. He compared them with the model.

Dacosta had let his smile unfold. "It disgusts me," Vendresse repeated between his teeth. "To become a forger, at my age. And that this should have to happen at a time when order has at last been restored in France. It disgusts me." His plump and agile fingers manipulated the composing stick.

"But what about the seal?" said Dacosta.

"*Nom de Dieu,* that's right, the seal."

"Don't worry," said Dacosta, "I know where I can have it stamped on."

"A forged seal?"

"A forged seal."

"But in that case, forged cards . . ."

"I could get hold of some, yes. But I shall be happy, so much happier, to have one made by you."

He was still smiling. Vendresse blushed, and his hands hesitated.

"You'll look after the kids?" said Dacosta suddenly. He was no longer smiling. His eyes were somber.

Vendresse's fingers resumed their work.

"Yes, you know I will. You need have no fear on that score."

"No fear . . ." said Dacosta. "They're Jewish too, and so is their mother. I wonder . . ."

Vendresse looked at him and said:

"Oh! After all!"

"You've already been wrong once," said Dacosta.

Vendresse finished his line in silence. His thick lips moved. He said — growled, rather:

"Wrong, wrong — it was the bad luck of stumbling on a son of a bitch like that pig Paars, that's all. You're off your nut. A woman, children! You can take my word and depart in peace: as long as the Old Man is there . . ."

"As long as he's there I won't be at peace, far from it. But you'll look after them? You won't let anything happen to them?"

"You'll find them fresh and rosy when you come back, I give you my word. Now go. I'll bring your card over to your place. I'll stay with your wife when you're gone."

Dacosta looked at his employer. He looked at him. He rubbed his mustache with one finger over and over again. A slight *tic* contracted the corner of his lips two or three times, while his right hand at the level of his hips executed a narrow, supple circle which expressed a kind of wavering renunciation. Vendresse saw all this and turned a little pale. Dacosta nevertheless managed to smile. Vendresse also managed to smile.

"All right," said Dacosta at last. "*Ça ira.*"[1]

He turned his back and went out.

Vendresse sat down on the bed of the press, his legs dangling, his chin in his hands.

∾

How had he suspected that he would get help from me? I have no idea. Perhaps because I always used to take Dacosta's side — against him. In any case it was my doorbell which he rang that morning. I was immediately struck by his eyes.

Vendresse had blue eyes; candid blue eyes. That morning they were black. I can't explain it. When you looked at them carefully they were blue as usual; but you would have thought they were black.

He said — just like that, without preamble:

"I want to print leaflets."

He sat down and panted, and began to rub his knees.

"Well," I said, "this is something new."

With a funny voice he said:

"Yes, this is something new."

[1] *Ça ira* (literally, "it will go"), expressing the resolve to see a thing through, has been almost a revolutionary slogan since 1789.

I wanted to give him time to reflect. "Well, really!" I said. "An old faithful like you? You, with your line of 'Pétain, save France,' 'Marshal, we are here,' 'Let's follow the Chief,' and 'France for the French'? Did I really understand you correctly, or are my ears playing me tricks?"

He said nothing. He just sat there quietly — motionless, a little alarming — looking at me. His eyes were black. I made up my mind.

"Leaflets," I said. "Good. It can be arranged. You know what you're risking?"

"Yes," he said.

"Oh," I went on, "not only being shot. But for instance, being tortured, to make you reveal my name — or others."

He hesitated a little and said:

"What do they do to you?"

I leaned back in my armchair, nonchalantly folding my arms and crossing my legs.

"Well," I said, "for instance, they prick you with little bits of burning wood under your fingernails. Or else they slowly crush your hand in a press. All sorts of things in that line. Or else they question you for two, three days without letup, without rest, under a blinding spotlight. Or else . . ."

"All right," he broke in, and appeared to meditate.

"I'm rather soft," he said, "not very courageous. Just the same, I think . . ." He looked above the door, as though he were searching for some object. He said, "Of course, the spotlight . . . shining in your eyes for three days . . ." He made a funny sound, with his thick lips. "One must become pretty near blind, eh?"

"Pretty near! I should think one might."

"And what a migraine, *nom de dieu!*" I remembered that he was subject to headaches, and understood why the thought of the spotlight tormented him (it was an evil which he knew). I then remembered that he was sensitive to cold and I said:

"They also plunge you in icy water, time after time, for hours."

"In icy water . . ." he repeated slowly. He nodded his head gently, looking off into space. He looked at me and said seriously, "Good, good, good . . ."

"*Ça ira?*" I said gently. His eyes struck me as blue.

"*Ça ira,*" he said.

I got up. I looked at him. "What has happened?"

He jumped. As if I had struck him in the face. He turned red, then pale. He looked at me with that expression of astonishment which people have, I am told, before they collapse with a bullet in the heart. Finally he said in a muffled voice, with his eyes on the floor:

"They've taken them away. The kids and her."

"Dacosta's?"

He nodded and looked up at me. "Dacosta's. Dacosta's wife and children. The kids one place, the mother somewhere else. She tried to jump out of the window. They prevented her. I . . ."

He was rubbing his knees. His eyes clung to mine. They appeared to me black as ink.

"What an ass I was. A miserable stupid ass. I believed in all those bandits. Dac had warned me. He had warned me, he had warned me . . . I could have . . . I should have . . . I would . . ."

He got up, began to pace the floor. In the light I saw that he was unshaven — unbelievable for him. He kneaded one side of his neck, slowly and heavily, causing it to turn red. Tears flowed one by one along his nose and vanished in his heavy mustache. It was comical and pathetic.

"I would have made them move, or sleep in

my place, or anything. But I didn't believe it. *Nom de dieu de nom de dieu,* how could anyone believe . . ."

He turned brusquely toward me:

"You know what he answered me?"

"Who?"

He raised his eyebrows and said, "Ah, yes . . ."

He resumed his pacing, stopped in front of the mirror, looked at himself, looked at his honest phiz all in tears, and began to laugh. It was rather awful.

"They came to my place first, the day before yesterday — no, three days ago. What havoc! My lead scattered everywhere and trampled on. Looking for what? The pleasure of destroying, that's all."

"Who? The Krauts?"

"Of course not! . . . They said to me, 'Go on! You, a veteran of Verdun!' They were just youngsters. I said, 'What has Verdun got to do with you?' They got mad. 'We're serving the Marshal!' 'So am I,' I said. They said, 'It doesn't look like it! Where is that Jew? He can't be far away since his things are here.' 'Look for him,' I said. The youngest one — a pimply-faced chap with a close haircut — said, 'Well, we don't give a damn. If we don't find him we'll take the wife and the brats.' I laughed. I said, 'Just try.' "

He stopped and looked at me. His little bit of a nose, under his glasses, was red.

"I said, 'Just try,' " he repeated and he looked at me. "And I was laughing," he said violently, and I heard his teeth grind. "Because I'm well acquainted with Tournier, the secretary of the Vieux de Verdun." He broke off and repeated, "I'm well acquainted with Tournier," in a choked voice and sneering at the same time. He uttered two dry little "Ha! Ha!'s" in rapid succession, half laughing, half in anger. He nodded his head. "I dashed over to see him, right away. With Dac's record — Verdun and the rest. I told him the whole story and I said, 'After all, eh? a *poilu* like him, that would be going pretty far. No danger, I hope?' He smiled and said, 'No, no, we'll fix that.' The following day, in fact, nothing happened. But yesterday . . ."

He stopped. I saw his back. An honest, broad, good-natured back, a little bent. I didn't see his hands, but from the movement of his arms I guessed that he was squeezing and unsqueezing them. He raised his head with a horselike motion (his plump, pink neck formed a roll of fat) and I heard him snort. He let his head fall and leaned on the desk. His back was still turned to me. He hammered the desk repeatedly with his little fist, which he had difficulty in closing, and I sensed the pent-up rage — the pent-up tears.

"It was the old baker woman . . ." he began, but his voice choked and he had to wipe his nose (we're funny animals: he was so comical, blowing through his little bit of a red nose, that I really had a hard time keeping myself from smiling. And yet my heart was wrung). "She was drumming at my door," he continued. "At seven in the morning, imagine! She kept repeating, 'Monsieur Vendresse! Monsieur Vendresse! They're taking them away!' I cried, 'Who?' but she didn't have to answer. I jumped out of bed. It was almost pitch dark. But after all, I had to dress!" he said as though he were afraid I would reproach him for this. His eyes darted right and left, and came to rest on a small canvas by Souverbie — three women done after the antique, three sleeping women — and such calm emanates from the very pure lines that it touches on the eternal, that it appears restful as death. Vendresse looked at the canvas — probably without seeing it — and his lips

187

trembled under the amber-stained mustache. It was as though he could not decide whether this serenity beyond time and space was a balm or an added torment to his aching heart.

"I arrived too late, naturally," he said. "The youngsters had already been taken away, God knows where. The mother . . ." He let out an odd cough, which I found painful: a little burst of laughter full of sobs and withheld cries. "She was shrieking, they were hitting her. in the face to make her stop. I ran, I shouted, but . . ." he raised his chin to show me a swollen bruise ringed with blue and brown . . . "I woke up on the edge of the sidewalk. The cars had left. The little pimply dark fellow was looking down at me, sneering. He said, 'You see, we tried.' He said something else in German, and the two Fritzes with him laughed too. They left me there. Some people helped me up, and took me to the pharmacist's. They didn't say anything. Nobody said anything."

"Naturally I ran to the Vieux de Verdun headquarters. Naturally there was nobody there. Naturally no Tournier. 'Away on a trip. We'll notify you.' I said, 'I want to see the President.' They looked at me with their eyes popping. 'The President?' I said — I shouted, 'Yes, the President, the

President!' I had forgotten that *he* was the President; I'm not joking — I had forgotten. And then I remembered: the Old Man . . . I continued to shout, I said I would see *any*body, any responsible person. They put me in a room. They made me wait half an hour, an hour, I don't know. I was ready to smash everything. Finally a fellow came; he looked annoyed, ceremonious and annoyed. I pulled out my record, I don't think I was able to talk very clearly, and he said, 'Yes, I know, Monsieur Tournier told me.' He raised his hands as though he were heartbroken. 'There's nothing to be done.' I began shouting again, and he went 'Tush . . . tush . . .' and finally he pulled out a piece of paper. It took me some time to understand. The fellow was explaining to me, but I just couldn't understand. 'You see, we can't take any action,' he said. He kept passing his finger across the paper, underlining a sentence, always the same one, but I just couldn't get the words into my head. '*In conformity with the terms of the above law, the members of* L'AMICALE *belonging to the Jewish race are to be expelled without further consideration or inquiry. Consequently they can no longer, (1) invoke . . .*" At last I understood and I turned the sheet over to see the signature. The

President's signature. The signature was there, all right. I saw it." He shouted, "I saw it!" Then in a voice which had become suddenly colorless he said, "There you are." He repeated, "There you are, there you are," and he raised toward me a wretched face with his mouth all twisted, and looking at me as if I had been Pétain himself he shouted in my face, a last time, "There you are!" and then his shoulders fell, his fists buried themselves in his eyes, and I went over to the window to let him cry himself out.

∾

I was very embarrassed. My impulse was to throw caution to the winds. But if I have managed to keep out of trouble and if none of those around me has been arrested, it is certainly thanks to this stubborn caution. It was embarrassing, but there was nothing for it but to tell him. I waited until he was more or less through wiping his nose and drying his eyes and I said:

"Look here, old man, I'm terribly sorry, but it won't work."

"What?" he asked.

"The leaflets. It's out of the question for you to print leaflets. You realize that they've got you

spotted. They're going to take every opportunity to make trouble for you. It would be dangerous for you, for me, and for all of us."

He looked at me for a moment and got up. He had a funny expression; it was the first time I had seen it on his face. I swear I did not recognize him. This was not the Vendresse I knew. He said calmly:

"All right. I understand. I'll go somewhere else. I'll go and see Dac's friends."

This time I couldn't help smiling.

"Dac's friends, Vendresse? The Bolsheviks?"

He did not smile, did not laugh. He said:

"Yes, the Bolsheviks. I'll go and see Coninck."

I stopped smiling, I blurted out a "No!"

"Why not?" He was on the doorstep.

"Come back," I said. "You can't go and see Coninck, nor any of the others. Coninck was caught."

There was a silence. He said slowly:

"Coninck was caught?"

"Yes," I said. "A long time ago. Three months, or more."

"Three months . . . but Dacosta . . ."

"Naturally," I said gently, "he didn't tell you. He couldn't tell *you* — at that time."

His face lengthened. He looked unbelievably unhappy. Well, I thought to myself, it's too bad. We'll find a way, a trick — something.

"Listen," I said aloud, "don't worry about it. I won't let you down. Go home and wait. I'll send someone to you. I promise you. But don't do anything foolish."

It's true, I added to myself (by way of excuse). It's better that I keep him under control.

∾

Necessity and circumstances give you ideas. I soon found the "trick" that was exactly the thing for Vendresse, and that did not involve too much risk: the mourning announcements. I discussed it with the fellows and we laughed no end at the idea, which struck us, moreover, as having all sorts of additional advantages: the certainty that these leaflets would be well distributed (how could the postal control check each one of the announcements which are mailed each day in tens of thousands?); the freedom Vendresse would have to print them in his own shop in perfect security during the first months, during which we would be stocking them (they would be put into circulation only later). We prepared thirty different

models — there was always the name in large characters, and below, in small type, the message that we wanted to put across. . . . We got a prodigious amount of fun out of this work. During those three months, as I had feared, Vendresse's place was searched on two occasions. They found nothing. And yet there were several bundles of announcements — some that were real and others that were false. But no one had the odd notion to read them.

At the end of the three months, when each of the thirty models had been printed in many thousands of copies, I intimated to Vendresse that he should lie low during the weeks when we would be distributing them. I promised him another job immediately after. I was perfectly at ease.

Labiche, my young contact agent, came every day to report on what was happening, within the framework of the group and on the fringe. One fine day, in the course of his report, he said, "Ah, Vendresse." "What about him?" I said. "He's been picked up."

My heart contracted. I immediately thought of Paars. "Somebody turn him in?" I asked.

"More than likely," said Labiche; "but I also think he blundered. He used to get into conversation with those who came to fetch the bundles in his shop — they told me so. He got in touch with

God knows what group. His place was searched the day before yesterday: the Gestapo . . . What a fool; after all, it was the third time, he should have been on his guard. . . . The dump was full of leaflets."

"Not ours?" I exclaimed in alarm.

"No, not ours."

We managed to trace him, although he had changed prisons three times. Naturally I had to move to a different address: I was not anxious to be subjected to the spotlight and the cold baths.

But he revealed nothing. We found out, moreover, that he had been tortured. He managed to get word to us. *"Tell the Sage* [that meant me] *not to worry. They didn't get anything out of me. The spotlight must be a joke: I've heard no mention of it. As for the baths, fortunately I pass out immediately. They've smashed my toes: right now my nails are dropping off."*

For seven months he remained in Fresnes. And then, Germany.

We had news of him again on two occasions, in '44 and in '45. Finally in April his comrades caught a glimpse of him for the last time: in a column — the camp was being evacuated. Frightfully emaciated. He could walk only with difficulty.

Since then, nothing. His pitiful body must be resting somewhere, in a ditch, along some road in Germany.

Little Madame Dacosta was gassed in Auschwitz. No news of the children. They are surely dead.

I know nothing of the father. I have heard that he was nabbed before Cassino. I am terribly uneasy at the thought of seeing him again. Sometimes I catch myself wishing he would not come back. I am very cowardly about certain things.

Vendresse's shop was taken over, after the arrest, by an old retired fellow, rotting with alcohol. He works with a strange apprentice, an adolescent whose head is too large for his body, sullen and taciturn, subject to sudden fits of anger that are talked about in the neighborhood.

Paars, after the liberation, was arrested and held for three days. But some very respectable people testified to his loyalty. Since the end of '43 he had contributed considerable sums to certain organizations. Moreover, he knows a great deal about matters concerning electrolytic copper. It seems that it would be difficult to do without him. He is a big shot in the Allocation Bureau, where he has things pretty much his own way.